ALIEN COMMUNICATIONS

Mr. Griffith:

We feel that one who every day must cope—and who copes successfully—with an exotic neurological disorder that causes him to suffer alarming hallucinations regularly, yet who notwithstanding this affliction remains on a tolerant, even friendly footing with his mind—we feel that such a person is eminently suited to fill the difficult position of guardian against the Öht.

"The Öht?" I asked.

The phone rang.

"They are, you might say, tourists," a voice began conversationally when I picked up the receiver. " 'Tourist' may not sound threatening, but consider what tourists are and what they do."

"Who is this?"

"Tourists," the voice went on, "show no respect. They track mud in a museum, eat potato chips in a temple. With their chewing gum and transistor radios they demoralize the natives."

It took a lot, these days, to make me scream. . . .

Ask your bookseller for the Bantam Spectra Special Editions you have missed:

STRANGE INVASION

Michael Kandel

BANTAM BOOKS
NEW YORK · TORONTO · LONDON · SYDNEY · AUCKLAND

STRANGE INVASION

A Bantam Spectra Book / September 1989

ISBN 0-553-28146-1

Published simultaneously in the United States and Canada

Bantam Books are published by Bantam Books, a division of Bantam
Doubleday Dell Publishing Group, Inc. Its trademark, consisting of the
words "Bantam Books" and the portrayal of a rooster, is Registered in
U.S. Patent and Trademark Office and in other countries. Marca Reg-
istrada. Bantam Books, 666 Fifth Avenue, New York, New York 10103.

PRINTED IN THE UNITED STATES OF AMERICA

O   0 9 8 7 6 5 4 3 2 1

Contents

Bonkers?

The spaceship, landing in my backyard, disguised itself as a bird feeder with birds. The birds—sparrows,
a couple of grackles, a cardinal—hopped and pecked
with such verisimilitude that I experienced a moment
of doubt. Had I seen a spaceship or hadn't I seen a
spaceship?

There was a knock at the back door; a man
dressed as a letter carrier gestured at me through the
glass. It occurred to me, my hand on the knob, that
perhaps I should not open to him. But this was silly.
If they could cross interstellar space, what protection
would a locked door give me? I took a breath and
opened.

"Mr. Griffith?" asked the mailman (really an
alien).

"Yes?"

"For you," he said, holding out a long, white envelope.

The letter was addressed to me, all right, but had
no stamp or postmark. I signed on the mailman's
clipboard, which I noticed was filled with signatures.

1

The envelope was made of the finest paper—stiff, parchmentlike. Was I supposed to open the envelope now? And was an answer expected? I was going to ask the mailman. But, looking up, I found that he was gone, and with him the bird feeder and the birds. One bird did remain, a house sparrow, but it was probably real.

Delicately, I held the letter, sniffed it. What did it contain? What could it possibly contain, seeing as I knew not a soul outside Earth. And not a soul outside Earth could be expected to know me. My name, after all, had never been on radio or television, whose signals travel into outer space. Once, at the age of nine, I was in the local paper, in the community activities—a Boy Scout picnic. I was awarded something, I forget what. A badge. Surely an extraterrestrial superrace would not follow our affairs *that* closely.

I picked up the phone and dialed Lucille. She was in.

"Hello, Wally," she said. "Having trouble?"

I explained that I had seen a spaceship and was debating whether or not to open a letter from it. That the spaceship had vanished, but not the letter.

"Well, open the letter," she said, cheerful. But I could feel her sympathy over the wire. Though a doctor, Lucille is a very caring person.

"All right," I said, and hung up.

I opened the letter. It read:

Mr. Griffith:

We feel that one who every day must cope—and who copes successfully, on the whole—with an exotic neurological disorder

that causes him to suffer alarming hallucinations regularly, yet who notwithstanding
this affliction remains on a tolerant, even
friendly footing with his mind—we feel that
such a person is eminently suited to fill the
difficult position of guardian against the Öht.

"The Öht?" I asked.

The phone rang.

"They are, you might say, tourists," a voice began
conversationally when I picked up the receiver.
" 'Tourist' may not sound threatening, but consider
what tourists are and what they do. The quick ruin
they work on an indigenous population."

"Who is this?"

"Tourists," the voice went on, "show no respect.
They'll track mud in a museum, eat potato chips in a
temple. With their chewing gum and transistor radios
they demoralize the natives."

I hung up. No run-of-the-mill attack, this. I called
Lucille again. She asked if I was keeping up the medication.

I was.

"Tell me how you feel, Wally. Are you upset?"

Not too. A little fluttery in the stomach. I didn't
know where all this was leading.

She thought a moment. "See it through. It may
lead to an insight. But no screaming."

It took a lot, these days, to make me scream. And
yet there was a time I screamed so much that screaming was like breathing. But the body still had its re-
flexes; it could knot up, panic, the panic feeding on
itself, the pulse going out of control. That was why I
needed the pills.

One must confront—*continued the letter in my hand*—not only radically different biological forms (and those in an incredible variety), but radically different cultures, concepts, value systems, weltanschauungs.

I looked up "weltanschauung" in my *Webster's*. The entry read, immediately after the definition, in tiny letters that flashed:

It is the sequence of conceptual-moral differences, rather than the biological, that tends to erode one's grip on reality.

"I suppose," I muttered, "that if I turn on the television, it will deliver the next sentence."

The television, as if to oblige, flicked on, though I was on the other side of the room and owned no remote control. The show was *Sesame Street*. Ernie tilted his head and said, in Ernie's reasonable way: "We're doing our best to communicate, Mr. Griffith."

"Communicate," I said, pulling up a chair. So far nothing was leaping out at me with fangs bared.

Ernie turned into a businesslike Dan Rather, who said: "Most individuals are unable to serve as a buffer between their species and the Öht for any practical length of time. Their personalities dissolve."

"Where do these Öht come from?" I asked.

The famous anchorman gave one of his charming-wise smiles. "From an unimaginably great number of unimaginably distant places. They are identified not by origin, and not in any political-territorial sense, but solely by what you might call their religion or sport—because their visiting of other seats of civilization has the elements both of a religion and a sport."

"What harm does this visiting cause?"

The screen presented a scene (in vivid color, though my set was black-and-white) of another planet. You could tell it was another planet because of the trees, which looked something like cactuses and something like asparaguses. The houses among the trees were golden stucco with expansive, sombrero roofs, giving the impression of a warm climate.

The people, human in appearance, mostly lay about. I saw no one working. No collective effort of any kind, not even for diversion (like card-playing). The scene shifted a little and closed in on two forms recumbent on a hill. One man had his elbows out and hands beneath his neck, gazing at the clouds. The other, a few feet away, parallel to him, was a corpse —so badly decayed that in places the skeleton gleamed white in the sun.

Then the camera went up and down the streets of a town, revealing, besides prodigious quantities of garbage, other examples of how these people failed to bury their dead. Hyena-type animals fed in the alleys; vulture-type birds were perched lethargically on the fences and gates.

There were a few old people, using canes as they walked, but not a child in sight. There were no couples. No pets. The large buildings—probably schools, hospitals, offices—were all unoccupied, and none of the vehicles were in operation. A caption ran along the bottom of the screen:

The Öht were here ten sidereal years ago.

I phoned Lucille again. "The hallucination is not only amazingly sustained," I said, "but instead of trying to scare me, it seems to be setting up one of those only-you-can-save-the-world stories. Do you think I've finally gone bonkers?"

"I wouldn't worry about going bonkers," said Lucille patiently, even though this was the third call in five minutes. "It's like fainting—some do and some don't. I can't say I understand what you're experiencing, Wally, but I don't believe you're in any danger."

"He's not," agreed my watch. "Not, at least, from us."

"Who's that?" Lucille asked.

I got sudden gooseflesh.

"You mean—Lucille, you heard it too?"

Lucille answered slowly. "Wally, are you telling me that something talked that shouldn't?"

"Hello, Lucille," said the watch.

"That's a watch talking?" Lucille asked.

"Yes, mine. That is, it's the people from outer space speaking through the watch. Are you there, Lucille?"

There was silence on her end.

"Perhaps someone's playing a trick on you," she said at last. But of course she knew that that could not be the case. I was alone—no friends, no enemies. Mr. Tribovich was my only acquaintance, inasmuch as I had been institutionalized from the age of ten, when the problem started, and was released less than a month ago.

The television said, loud, in the voice of the president of the United States: "Whether or not you can save your world, Mr. Griffith, is open to question. The odds, actually, are against it. Only one in ten guardians, at best, in this corner of the galaxy, manages to keep the Öht out."

"Wally," said Lucille, "I think I'd better come over."

"You're hearing it too, Lucille?"

"I'll be there in fifteen minutes, a half hour, depending on the traffic." She hung up.

"Your sanity, though you maintain an understandable skepticism toward it," the president continued, "is all the more stable for having been so severely and repeatedly assaulted."

A sketch on my desk doodle pad caught my eye. Animated: another special effect. Depicted was a clown on a tightrope, holding his umbrella out at this angle, that angle, while his polka-dotted body twisted to avoid the fruit thrown at him.

"So we get discouraged—demoralized—by these tourists from Planet X," I said. "So everything goes to pot for ten years, or maybe twenty. Won't the next generation pick up the ball?"

It wasn't the television that demonstrated, this time, but an entire living room wall. The pictures were breathtakingly lifelike, they were more than pictures. It was as if the wall had been replaced by a window to other worlds. Several examples, following in quick succession, made the same point. Apparently, the kind of demoralization caused by the Öht was so profound, it led to nothing less than complete extinction. The ghost towns, ghost cities, and ghost suburbs that I saw were a theater only for weeds and rodents.

"A one-in-ten shot," I said, clearing my throat, "isn't much."

BETTER, HOWEVER, THAN NOTHING

—responded the wall, in block letters.

"What are you, then?" I asked. "Superheroes giving a hand to the underdog?"

CONSERVATIONISTS

—was the answer, this time in the form of spots in the air, before my eyes.

Feeling giddy, I went outside and took a deep breath, standing on the front-door mat. It was a fine spring day. But I didn't put my trust in anything in sight—not the fence, not the lawn, not even the warm, yellow sun.

A squirrel flapped its tail and addressed me from a limb of the old maple near the driveway. Its voice was deep and resonant. "The reason we cannot do more is that greater interference on our part would bring the whole matter to the attention, eventually, of those whose attention is best avoided."

"How do you *do* that?" asked a lady who was passing by.

I smiled at her and shrugged.

"That's some trick," she said, stopping.

"Thank you."

She looked at me, then at the tree. (Wires? Speakers?)

I nodded, smiling. She saw, finally, that she would receive no explanation, so returned the smile and reluctantly went on her way.

"Now, that lady," I said to myself, "would have got no farther than the spaceship. She'd be gibbering."

A kid on a bicycle rode up the driveway, handed me a supermarket circular from his basket, and left. Expecting a message, I opened the circular. A sale on chicken. Wax beans, dental floss, aluminum foil. Nothing from the aliens. I felt stupid.

Lucille drove up. She came stumbling out of the car, hair loose, face white. It alarmed me to see her in such a state. In my life she was the one who steadied, not who needed steadying.

"They spoke to me," she gasped, gripping my shoulder.

"The watch, you mean, over the phone."

"No, the car radio! And from the signs!"

"Lucille, take one of my pills."

She shook her head. "They questioned me about you. As your doctor. About your history. Can this really be happening?" She held on to me. "You know, Wally, this must be what it's been like for you all these years. I don't know how you took it."

I led her in and poured her a cup of coffee. "Actually, this is not what it's been like. The usual stuff is monsters, grinning heads, creepy things."

"Some of the Öht," remarked the refrigerator, making Lucille jump and give a strangled cry, "are frightening to behold."

"Wally," said Lucille, "I'll have one of your pills."

She downed it with her coffee, not even blowing on the coffee to cool it off.

"Excuse me," I said to the refrigerator, and to the room in general. "If you could limit yourselves, with this communicating, to one object, such as a television set, it would be a lot easier on us, especially on Lucille here, who isn't as accustomed as I am to hearing and seeing things."

"We like to keep moving," said the refrigerator.

I gave that some thought.

"In order that whoever it is you're afraid of won't get a fix on you?"

The refrigerator nodded. "If we stay on one channel, we leave what you might think of as footprints." The newspaper on the table between us unfolded by itself. The lead article read:

Not that we're doing anything to be ashamed of, you understand. On the contrary. It's a question of jurisdiction.

"And the spaceship was in your backyard?" Lucille asked in a whisper, going over to the window.

I explained to her how it descended, assumed the form of a feeder complete with birds, and vanished. After vanishing, it could have assumed, of course, some other form. It could have become one of the trees out back.

"How many trees do you have?" she asked, looking out the window.

"Five or six."

"Which is it? Five or six?"

I wasn't sure. Who counts the trees in his backyard?

"Your friends from outer space," she told me, "like your psychological profile. They call it favorable. The only problem with you, according to them (I read this, God help me, off a cigarette billboard on the expressway), is that you are a little too self-centered."

"Self-centeredness," a voice gurgled from the sink, "is not a good quality in a guardian. A guardian should be devoted to his species."

Lucille said she needed to lie down. I took her upstairs, made her comfortable, kept my fingers crossed that she wouldn't be bothered by any more communicating, then went outside to see which of the trees, if any, was a spaceship. They all had the feel of trees. Bark. I encountered no force field. My neighbor, Mr. Tribovich, called out to me from his yard, over the fence. "How you?"

"Fine," I shouted.

"Time again to rake the leaves," he called happily, gesturing. Mr. Tribovich was always happy.

"Right."

"And plant the garden."

Actually, the landlord, old Mr. Forbes, had said no to gardens. But Mr. Tribovich took me for the owner.

"Everybody should have a garden," Mr. Tribovich called. "You get married, you have a garden. Eat better." He smacked his pot belly. As far away as I was, I could hear the smack.

"The first invasion," said a voice in my ear, "is next Thursday, fifty miles west of Bucaramanga, in Colombia. Just before noon."

"By invasion," I said, looking around for the speaker, "you mean the Öht?" (Was it an insect, this time, a mite? Or was it my earwax now talking to me?)

"Yes. Fifty miles west of Bucaramanga, you'll see from the road a high meadow. It's less than a mile north—within sight—of Barrancabermeja. Try not to be late."

The voice, I had the impression, was saying good-bye. I was relieved that the aliens were departing, but I had a few questions yet. I asked hurriedly, running back inside: "About this guardian business . . . is there any danger to me personally if I do—whatever it is I'm supposed to do? And what is it, exactly? How do I keep the Öht off? Do you have some ray gun to give me? And suppose I don't choose to be a guardian?"

I ran up to see how Lucille felt. She was sound asleep, snoring, unaccustomed to the drug. The bedroom wallpaper design wiggled into words.

You are not given a choice in the matter.
Guardians, physically, run no personal risk.
Use psychology, not force, against the Öht.

I ran back down. "How can I use psychology when they're not even human?" I picked up the phone for the answer.

The voice came from a great distance. The aliens were definitely leaving. "Everybody's human, Mr. Griffith."

"But wait! How am I supposed to get to this Baranga—"

"Bucaramanga."

"By plane, or what? And who's paying? It costs a bundle to fly to South America."

Only a dial tone.

There was a knock at the door. The mailman again, the same one. He gave a short salute, handed me another unstamped letter, and dispersed in a poof of reddish brown dust.

The envelope contained a round-trip ticket to Bogotá. There was also a note, which said:

Good luck! Hope you can save your world.
We're attaching a peripheral to you, to assist
in the details. Please remember, for the sake
of all concerned, to keep as low a profile as
possible.

"I don't even know Spanish," I muttered.

The words on the paper vanished and in their place was a cartoon. Tom and Jerry. Tom was chasing Jerry as usual, but ran on tiptoe—past Spike, the big bulldog asleep in his doghouse. The bulldog, I guessed, represented those whose attention is best avoided.

The page went blank.

I went and woke Lucille. I told her that the men from outer space were gone.

She blinked. It took her a moment to get her bearings. She propped herself up, shook her head to clear it. "Maybe we've both gone off the deep end."

"Lucille," I said, pointing to the window. Here was an opportunity to test the deep-end hypothesis. "Do you see anything out of the ordinary over in that direction?"

She shook her head. She didn't. She looked at me. "What do *you* see, Wally?"

A hairy potato sitting on the windowsill. The potato, like a dwarf, had a large head and diminutive arms and legs. Its face, dirt-brown, lumpy, contained a mouth that went from ear to ear (except there weren't ears) and was twisted, among bristles of beard, sardonically. The small and puffy eyes regarded me with an evil gloat.

"Nothing much," I said. "A normal hallucination."

She got up, examined my watch, tested the telephone, and opened and closed the refrigerator a couple of times. "I have to get back to the office," she said at last, still looking around nervously. "Maybe none of this happened."

But the airplane ticket was entirely real. She called and confirmed the flight.

"What do you think I should do, Lucille?"

"I don't know," she said. "But if we're going to be invaded by alien tourists, and these Conservationists say it's up to you to keep them away . . . To tell the truth, Wally dear, I keep thinking I'm . . ." But she didn't finish. She told me to keep up the medication and left.

I watched her drive off, then went to the dictionary and looked up "peripheral." The definition didn't help. I had a sinking feeling that soon an awful lot would be expected of me. I had been out in the world for not even a month, and just the job of being an average person, independent, taking care of myself from day to day, still seemed, sometimes, more than I could handle.

Also, it disturbed me, my reaction to seeing Lucille asleep on my bed. I was churned up about that, even with the pill. What kind of ideas was I getting?

Barrancabermeja

My brain, due to some abstruse metabolic anomaly that in turn is due to some gene not being where it should be on the chromosome, produces two or three chemicals that are powerful hallucinogens. These chemicals have impressively long names, and I've seen their structures put up on the blackboard. The doctors at the hospital were anxious to show me that the things I was seeing and hearing were in reality purely molecular. It was amusing, sometimes, to see a pink bat perched on Dr. Gross's shoulder as he explained. The bat and the doctor, opponents on either side of the existence question, were equally smug.

I hate the pink bats, because they actually bite and can cause welts (or blisters). Power of suggestion or no power of suggestion, I dodge when attacked. Who likes pain? It presents problems, however, when I'm out in public or, worse, being examined by a psychologist. Sudden, unexplained movements make people apprehensive.

A pink bat appeared on the plane while they were serving food. With the tray in front of me and a fat woman like a wall of pillows between me and the aisle, I had no room to maneuver. The illusion approached slowly; it knew it had me. The damned thing sank its fangs into my wrist. All I could do, in revenge, was pretend it wasn't there. I lifted my coffee cup and sipped.

It's true that even without the medicine very little fazes me. Human beings, I've read, are miracles of adaptability, and I suppose I'm a case in point. My Aunt Penny—who visited me shortly after I was released from Rosedale, and whom I haven't seen since—complained that I was "unemotional." Dr. Gross, on the other hand, said that he envied me my equanimity. I looked the word up: a good word.

The biggest problem about my condition is that every now and then something really peculiar happens and then I have no way of telling whether or not it's just my chemicals—those cortical alkaloids—acting up. If a lion escaped from a zoo and I saw it on a street corner, I'd probably ignore it or try to walk straight through it.

The probability of seeing a lion on a street corner is low, it's negligible. But in a foreign country, in a less familiar, less citified area of the Earth, a lion on a street corner might not be so farfetched. I worried about this, getting off the plane at Bogotá. How would I know an Öht when I saw one?

I managed well, much better than I thought I would, with the business of finding and checking into a hotel. I didn't have to use my phrase book or pocket dictionary once. Everyone spoke English. They treated me like an old friend. It wasn't until I was in bed, with the blanket tucked comfortably under my chin, that I realized that no one had spoken English to me. I had spoken Spanish the whole time, with the ease of a native.

The next morning I returned to the airport and took a plane to Bucaramanga. During the flight the air was crystal clear. Underneath us, one town after another passed by, all picturesque, nestled between the mountains. They looked like kingdoms in a fairyland. But in Bucaramanga the sky was overcast and the air muggy. My hotel room had roaches. Obscenities were written in the toilet stall at the end of the hall.

The next day—Wednesday, the day before the invasion, according to the visitors from outer space —I had a few hours to kill, after breakfast, until the bus left for Barrancabermeja, so I went for a walk in the city. I saw two eighteenth-century churches, pastel yellow and white, and the Bucaramanga University, a collection of massive gray buildings and green parks. There were traffic lights, stores, and even air pollution.

I bought a hat and sunglasses. Then a pack of scrawny children attached themselves to me. They wanted money. Not that I objected to giving them something—but I was afraid they might jump me at the sight of my wallet, like piranha at the smell of blood. They were scruffy, muddy, and looked amoral around the eyes and mouth.

To shake them off, I went into a post office. I mailed Lucille a postcard depicting a coffee plantation, coffee being one of the department of Santander's claims to fame. "Wish you were here," I wrote in English. The gamins, I saw, were waiting for me outside. I asked a clerk if there was a bakery nearby. Indeed yes, he replied, just around the corner. So I led my band of predators to the bakery. The baker began to curse at them, shaking his fist, but I raised my hand and presented him with a large, crisp note.

"Order what you like, go ahead," I said to the children, who after a moment of hesitation charged the counter. I made a quick exit.

There were no followers when I walked through the drizzle to the bus station. I was proud of myself. Perhaps, after all, I might be able to deal with the invaders, too, when they came. Avoid confrontation, be creative.

The bus took four and a half hours. By the time we arrived, I was too exhausted to think of supper. The jostling, the fumes, the crowd of people in the seats and aisle, the noise had worn me out. All I wanted was to get into bed. But my room was too hot. The fan didn't help a bit—and the top sheet couldn't be flung off because of the mosquitoes.

What if I overslept Thursday? Would that be the end of the world? I kept checking my watch. Neon snakes, smelling of sauerkraut, slithered on and off the furniture. Or voices called my name, with monster laughter. I wished I could talk to Lucille. But she had said to me: "Wally, you've done beautifully on your own. And now you'll be on your own in a way that would challenge anyone. I know you can do it—I have faith in you—but it will be easier, better, if you let go of my hand." I was to call, she said, only in dire emergencies.

Speaking to Lucille in my thoughts and imagining her answers made me feel better. But sleep didn't come. How would I function tomorrow, without sleep? I dozed, on and off, until the dawn. At dawn I got up, afraid that if I stayed in bed, I might fall into a deep sleep, with my fatigue, and miss the invasion. I went out to have a look at Barrancabermeja.

Barrancabermeja was an interesting town, full of boats and docks along the wide river—the Magdalena—and there were mountains in the background, on both sides, but one could not call the place charming or picturesque. It was industrial. Smokestacks, a big oil refinery. The houses on the perimeter of the factories, crammed together, were squalid. I was reminded a little of Pittsburgh.

I had breakfast at a greasy spoon on the waterfront. Killed time reading a newspaper. Drank coffee, dozed, checked my watch—until a man came over to my table.

"You are a salesman," he said.

I shrugged and invited him to sit down.

He introduced himself as Vélez—I didn't catch the first name—from Vélez, where he had a plantation on the Suárez. Mr. Vélez had a lot to say about taxes. Experiencing tax difficulties, he was interested in textile production in Barrancabermeja, and believed that the future of northern Colombia was water power.

My name? I made something up. Mr. Vélez observed that although I spoke with barely an accent I was obviously not of this part of the world.

"How can you tell?" I asked.

"The cast of your skin shows that you are unaccustomed to the heat. In Maracaibo, once, I met a sailor from Finland with exactly such skin."

The heat was in fact becoming uncomfortable. The sun, rising in the sky, had already reached a surprising height. But we were not far, I remembered, from the Equator.

I admitted that I was not a native. I came from central Argentina, I told Mr. Vélez: the Río Negro province, Viedma. Interested, he asked me question after question about the area's commerce. I excused myself; I had an appointment, I said. He shook my hand and gave me his card. He looked at me expectantly, waiting—I realized—for my card in exchange. I explained that I had no card.

"You are a singular salesman," he said, shaking my hand again. "But I wish you every success in Santander."

"Thank you."

The high meadow was in sight. On the other side of the smokestacks and the bridge, it faced the harbor, overlooking the Magdalena. To get to the bridge, I had to pick my way through a maze of narrow streets, but every choice I made proved correct. (My peripheral at work, I guessed.) The sun overhead was brutal—or it may have been the humidity—but the hat and sunglasses helped. I removed my jacket and slung it over my shoulder.

The meadow above Barrancabermeja, when I approached it, turned out to be a cemetery. It was a quarter to eleven, so I had about an hour to wait. I sat on a broken bench and listened to myself pant. Boats honked. The factory next to the refinery rumbled.

A black skeleton came out of the ground and walked toward me. "That's fine," I said. "Just stay conventional, or I won't be able to tell you from the Öht—whatever it is they look like." I assumed the Öht would be un-Halloweenlike.

Later, a beetle-green gourd came out of the ground. I frowned. The real thing, this time, or a false alarm? I got up and accosted the gourd. "Are you an Öht?"

"I'm a Chivri and a Believer," snapped the gourd. "And if you crowd me or become rude, I'll give you a fillip you won't soon forget." It spoke with such firmness that I automatically retreated a step and assumed a head-lowered posture of respect. This creature was definitely un-Halloweenlike.

"Excuse me," I asked, "but are you here as a tourist?"

"We're going to have a party," replied the gourd.

And, in fact, I saw that several more gourds had emerged from the earth. They were green—in different shades: olive, pea, moss. What puzzled me the most was that they were arriving from below instead of from above. Materializing through some kind of space warp?

I call them gourds—actually they were bipeds, but one tended not to notice the legs, which were short and colorless. There were fringes and flaps in places on the body, but it was hard to say whether this was clothing or anatomy.

I cleared my throat. "Excuse me, but, as you can see, the town here isn't much to look at. I doubt that there are any entertainment spots in it. And around and about, for miles, all you'll find are dirt farms."

"Whoopee," said the gourd, and moved on.

It was followed by hundreds of gourds. And hundreds more appeared behind those hundreds. I watched from the hill as a stream of bobbing green balloons wound its way down and across the bridge toward the Barrancabermeja harbor and refinery.

What specifically the Chivris had in mind, in the way of partying, I didn't know. I hurried after, feeling ineffectual. Apparently I had failed to seize whatever opportunity I had had. Yet what could have been done at the cemetery (it all happened, was all happening, so quickly) and what could be done, now, against this strange horde of pleasure-seekers?

Downtown, the gourds were partying in a recognizable fashion. They ate, laughed, drank, told jokes, sang, danced, embraced. I was relieved to see that in every respect their activities were confined to themselves. They had even brought their own refreshment with them. The main thing: they ignored completely the citizens of Barrancabermeja, who stood riveted, gawking.

Although I was ignorant of the biology of the gourds, it was soon plain to me—and must have been to everyone—that the embracing that was going on was of the type best done behind closed doors and not in public view. The gourds were shameless; they threw themselves into their merrymaking with an abandon that made one's mouth fall open.

Hesistantly I approached a Lincoln-green gourd who stood alone. "Sir or Madam," I began, afraid of a fillip, "excuse me for interrupting." The gourd, I now saw, was engaged in self-abuse; shuddering with pleasure, it probably could not have spoken, just then, even if it wanted to. I withdrew, averting my eyes, and tried another gourd, one drinking.

"I don't mean to intrude," I said.

"Want some?" The gourd, more khaki than green, offered me its bottle.

"Thank you, no. I wonder if you could tell me something?"

The gourd turned away—to pick up what resembled a wedge of chocolate cake. It ate, moaning softly with pleasure.

"I don't mean to intrude," I said, "but I was wondering what the occasion is, for the party."

The gourd belched. I had never heard such relish in a belch. The creature put its soul into it, prolonged it, practically sang it.

"Excuse me," I tried again, but an electric shock sent me sprawling on cobblestones.

"Don't crowd," warned the gourd, briefly stern.

My hair stood on end a little, and my fingers and toes tingled. There was no real pain involved, but the fillip left me edgy, as if I had consumed too much caffeine. My heart flopped now and then, out of rhythm. No more questions, I decided.

The Chivris—or Öht—were a humorless bunch in spite of their revelry. Officials of some kind, was my guess, on vacation. They probably had no fun for years on end, working long hours, without coffee breaks, in gray offices, for taskmasters stonier than themselves—and then they were given a week to blow off steam.

I got up and dusted myself off. I had a sore throat—from speaking Chivri'ese, an unusually guttural tongue—and the sweat trickling down my forehead made my eyes sting. The Colombian sun was fierce.

Green gourds filled the street; they filled the streets in every direction. Even the hillsides around the river were crawling with the invaders. And everywhere they were doing the same thing: seizing the moment.

Meanwhile more and more, thousands, tens of thousands, were emerging from the cemetery above the Magdalena, each Chivri determined to make the most of its short vacation. In my mind's eye I saw them spreading out over the countryside, like an infection, until they reached Bogotá, the Pacific, the Caribbean. I saw them overrunning the continent, the hemisphere, the world.

But why Earth? What attractions did we have to offer? Perhaps Earth was simply a more primitive, less civilized place for them—where they could let their hair down, so to speak, without worrying about witnesses. (An evolutionarily inferior witness doesn't count. A dog watching is the same as no one watching.)

I went to the Barrancabermeja bus depot to take the next bus back to Bucaramanga, bitterly chewing my defeat. What had the Conservationists said? One chance in ten? What a mistake, on their part, to have chosen me, of all people, to serve as guardian. But maybe these Öht would leave soon, on their own, and there would be no lasting damage.

The depot was packed inside and out with partying gourds. There would be no transportation today. An old bus that stood off to the side also had been taken over. I observed with alarm that there were people in it, not only gourds, and that the people were partying, too. Was this the beginning of the fatal demoralization that the Conservationists spoke of?

One woman had removed her clothes. She was pouring wine on her head, letting it run down her hair and down her brown body. It took me some effort to look away, having not seen a naked woman before, except in magazines.

There was no question but that the attitude of the gourds was catching. Seeing a person enjoying himself totally, wholeheartedly, without guilt, the spectator begins to ask himself why not. I was in the midst of a seething orgy.

I left the depot, appropriated a bicycle in an alley,

and headed east on the road to Bucaramanga. Then I was in a driving rain. Soaked, I continued biking. The rain stopped, the sky grew brighter, but the sun was unable to break through the clouds. Mist billowed up from the surface of the road. It was like traveling in a Turkish bath; hard to breathe. Buildings took shape in the mist ahead—but how could this be Bucaramanga already? I had been pedaling less than an hour.

It was the Barrancabermeja refinery. Somehow I had become turned around. Or else, in the rain and mist, I had got onto side roads without knowing it and made a circle. To my right, a group of gourds danced ecstatically in a field of mud, and humans —of Indian extraction—were clapping for them, singing.

Back toward Bucaramanga I pedaled, eastward, wanting desperately to be home again, to see Lucille. Would she be disappointed in me? (And how long would it take the invasion to reach us, if it kept going?) Suddenly I knew that I was not riding in the direction I intended. This had to be the work of the peripheral. Would it keep returning me, by the scruff of the neck, to my duty?

"The Conservationists," I muttered, "don't put much stock in free will."

I jumped off the bicycle, let it fall, and bolted into the woods, improvising. Acting on impulse might shake whatever was monitoring me. The woods gave way to a field that contained an unfamiliar crop (probably an illegal drug), and then there were more woods. The underbrush became so thick, I could move forward only with the utmost exertion.

It occurred to me, as I waded, that there could be poisonous snakes on the ground. I had no way of knowing, placing my feet blind, since the foliage shut out everything. So I climbed a tree, frightening little lizards off the bark, and rested, in a crotch high up, exhausted. It rained again; a thin stream of water fell on my head, as from a spigot; but I was already soaked, so it didn't matter. Would I get malaria from this? Yellow fever?

A sound like someone clearing his throat. I looked up and saw, on a limb not far from me, a gorgeous tropical bird with a huge beak.

"You're beautiful," I said, "but funny-looking."

It turned its head and regarded me with one eye.

"From your point of view, I suppose so," said the bird.

I was disappointed. "Oh, for a moment I thought you were real."

After a pause, as if considering what I had said, the bird spoke again. "And what caused you to change your mind?"

I smiled. This was a logical figment. "Birds don't talk. And besides, I frequently see things that aren't there."

The bird's head feathers shifted slightly, giving the impression that it raised its eyebrows (of course birds don't have eyebrows). "Birds *do* talk," it said. "They have been talking since the Jurassic. Though, I grant you, what they have had to say in that time has not been earthshaking." It made a clucking, whir-ring noise. "What surprises *me*," it went on in a dif-ferent tone, half to itself, "is that you deny that birds talk and yet you speak our language impeccably."

"Birds have a language?"

The rain let up, and the stream of water, thank goodness, stopped funneling onto my head. But the forest was filled with the pat-pat of drops falling from leaf to leaf. The pat-pat would probably go on all day, even if the sun came out, there were so many leaves. I felt drowsy, but my perch was too uncomfortable to allow me to sleep, and my wet clothes chafed.

On the bough near me, the bird, brilliant red, yellow, white, and black, shook its beak. "If we're going to converse," it said, "we ought to introduce ourselves. My name is Ramphastidus and I'm a toucan." It added, in an aside, "The beak, which appears to amuse you, is for eating fruit. You are probably accustomed to finches, who eat seed."

I introduced myself and in a few words gave the toucan my story. The toucan was skeptical but polite, interrupting only once, to ask what outer space was.

"Too abstract for me," it said, after I attempted to explain about vacuums. "I don't see how an object can travel through *nothing*. There has to be something there, you know, to buoy it."

What language was I speaking? It seemed American English, but, then, so had Colombian Spanish at first. Were my lips puckered, to make whistles? Did my tongue trill? And—another question, assuming that this was not a hallucination—did all birds have one language, or did each species possess its own, like different countries? Could I be speaking toucanese?

The toucan was disgusted by the image of massive, unbridled pleasure-seeking. "Nothing could be more foreign," it said, "to the nature of birds."

I pointed out that birds, however, did have the reputation of being frivolous and impractical. Free spirits. Singing while others worked.

The toucan retorted, with a sound close to a snort, that of the creatures of the animal kingdom the birds were unquestionably among the most industrious. "You will not find a bird sunning itself." A prodigious amount of food had to be consumed, each day, to supply the energy for the labor of flight. Nests had to be built, fledglings nurtured. Migration twice a year, for many, for thousands of miles.

"Our life," said Ramphastidus, "is a constant struggle. Read Darwin, read Marx."

"You're familiar with Marx?" How could a toucan in a jungle possibly know Marx? (How, without hands, could it turn the pages of *Das Kapital*?)

"I happen to be a Marxist," said Ramphastidus, raising his beak with pride.

"What possessed you to become a Marxist?" I asked.

"In this part of the world, one is either a Marxist or a scoundrel."

True, I had forgotten how much injustice there was throughout Central and South America. Banana republics, military juntas. This toucan could have learned its Marxism from some Communist guerrilla passing through. Perhaps the guerrilla, sitting with his back against a tree, had perused *Das Kapital*, and the toucan, on a branch, looked over the man's shoulder.

"The political history of our land," the toucan went on, "is a litany of violence and oppression. And of exploitation by foreign powers."

"You do sound like a Marxist," I admitted.

Ramphastidus commenced a speech. The rising proletariat of Colombia. Health and literacy problems. The need for collectivization of agriculture. Modern farm machinery. Mining. As the bird talked, I thought how different this approach to life was from that evident in the holiday rampage of the green gourds. Here you had duty, a sense of high purpose wedded to sober realism, and the sacrifice of self for the common good; there—nothing but eat, drink, and be merry, the gratification of the flesh.

A giant black spider reached for me from below, but I paid no attention to it. Disappointed, it vanished. My pulse, however, had gone up. In the excitement of the day, I had completely forgotten to take a pill. I fished the plastic vial out of my jacket pocket; not having a cup, I swallowed the pill dry.

The toucan looked at me sharply. "Are you an addict?"

I explained my problem and the effect it had on the sympathetic nervous system. But in whatever language it was that I was using I couldn't find the necessary medical terms, so the explanation came out lame.

"I don't abide drugs," said Ramphastidus, shifting from one foot to another on the bough, as if preparing to fly away. "They are a waste of productivity."

A light went on in my brain. "Ramphastidus," I said, "I don't think you appreciate the danger of these gourds. They're invading. In a couple of weeks, unchecked, they might spread their influence over the entire country and farther."

The bird grew still. "I'm only a toucan," it said quietly. "If you're appealing to me, as a Marxist, to do something, I must remind you that I'm only a toucan. Toucans cannot take up arms."

"You can speak, though. You could deliver speeches."

"In no tongue that men, much less beings from outside our ecosystem, would understand."

"But suppose I take care of that difficulty."

I reasoned: the peripheral overcame language barriers. Though attached to me, it might agree to extend its action to my deputies, who would be, after all, fighting on the same side.

The idea was to have Ramphastidus lecture not the people of Barrancabermeja, but the Öht. I thought, putting myself in the shoes of a tourist bent on carousal, that there could be nothing more objectionable than having a persistent, sour presence standing over one and preaching civic duty.

"But there are millions of these gourds, you said," Ramphastidus pointed out.

"A single toucan would have a problem reaching such an audience, of course, but surely there are other toucans of your acquaintance who share your political views." I crossed my fingers.

Ramphastidus nodded.

I urged the bird to round up its Marxist colleagues immediately. We would meet in an hour—there was no time to lose—at the harbor bridge. Ramphastidus, crying, "Workers of the world, unite!" took to the air gracefully, while I scrambled down the tree, skinning my shins. But would I be able to find my way back to the road and the bicycle?

A sign that I had not noticed before, a warped, weather-beaten board nailed to a dead tree, contained an arrow. The paint was badly faded, and the nails made long drip-stains of rust in the wood, indicating that the sign had been there for ages and was forgotten. But, beginning to suspect the devious ways of the peripheral, whose creators were masters of illusion, I guessed that the arrow was entirely for my benefit, so I followed it.

There were other arrows like the first, at convenient intervals. Sure enough, they led me back to the bicycle, which was not lying in the middle of the road as I had left it, but instead stood neatly off to the side, propped against a fence post. The chain and pedals had been oiled.

After five or ten minutes of hard pedaling I came to a sign that said:

> **BULLHORNS**
> **UP AHEAD**
> 40% OFF

How could there be, in Barrancabermeja, a demand for bullhorns great enough to support a business devoted exclusively to the sale of them? This seemed so unlikely that I dismissed the reality of the store, when I reached it, and rode past; but suddenly the bicycle swerved onto the store's gravel driveway.

What did I need bullhorns for?

But of course: the toucans would have a problem making themselves heard over the merriment. (And how exactly, I wondered, would the peripheral handle the translating? Would my toucans do their exhorting in Chivri'ese? Would the gourds understand toucanese? Or would the sound waves be altered appropriately between them? Not that it mattered.)

The man who appeared, finally, after I rang the bell on the counter, was large and swarthy. Although it was late in the afternoon, he looked like he had just got up, and with a hangover. I asked, trying to sound all business, if I could use a credit card. His answer was a very slow, sarcastic smile. I told him that I required a considerable quantity of bullhorns, maybe a couple hundred. "Even at forty percent off," I explained, "I wouldn't have the cash for that." (But did the man stock that many bullhorns?) "Also," I said to him, "if at all possible, I'd like them to be on the small side. I mean, with small handles. The handles should be small enough for a toucan, for example, to use."

I offered to write a check. He said nothing, only smiled his nasty smile. I went cold. What if the man insisted on cash? The fate of the world could depend on those bullhorns. Desperation gave me strength. I felt suddenly capable of breaking the law, of killing, even, if it was necessary. The man outweighed me, had big shoulders, but what was there to lose? What did a punch in the face matter, giving it or receiving it, with the end of the human race looming?

"Where are the bullhorns?" I shouted, and pushed the man out of the way, my hand sinking in his belly.

He did not resist. Possibly he took me for a gangster-bandit, who would be armed. Colombia, after all, is overrun with gangster-bandits.

The bullhorns were in a long building in the back that smelled of chickens. And there was feather fluff on the floor. This must have been an egg farm before the man went into bullhorns.

I cursed the man and told him to start loading the bullhorns immediately onto his pickup truck, which I had seen in the driveway, and to get his family to help him, since it was imperative that I be at the bridge within the hour.

But would the truck work? Was there enough gas? Would the toucans show up? My forehead was covered with sweat.

And Lord knows how much in the meantime the Öht had multiplied.

Bacchanal

At Rosedale, Cliff liked to hit me in the shoulder, hard, with the knuckles, when he greeted me, so that I had a constant bruise there. For him, that was like a handshake. I hated being hit, but knew that it was out of the question to return blow for blow. Once I saw him shoved by an orderly, a beer-bellied character with a tattoo and war stories who didn't remain with us long. Not much of a shove, either, but it triggered a blind rage. Red eyes, foaming mouth, clawing fingers.

These gourds—I could sense it—were like that. Any physical threat to them, anything so much as resembling a threat, and you'd be blasted. Retaliation totally out of proportion.

So when the pickup truck, turning a corner, confronted a wall of cavorting green, I told Carlos (the teenage son of the bullhorn seller) to stop and not to honk. There was no way we could reach the bridge, our rendezvous point with the toucans.

"They will move aside," said Carlos. "I will go slow."

"Don't try, *please*," I said. For an object as large as a truck, the fillip would have tremendous voltage.

Why was Carlos not speechless at the sight of a sea of aliens? Perhaps he thought that this was a convention. And it was: businessmen away from home.

I got out of the truck, searching the sky. The clouds were cream as the sun went down. The smokestacks of the plant by the refinery, tranquil above the seething invasion, turned a golden yellow. We could all drop dead for all the smokestacks cared. Where, where were the toucans?

Carlos was gone. Then I saw him. In the street, he had a bottle to his lips, and his chest was bare. I ran to retrieve him. The boy was not even fifteen. But in the crush someone pulled my head to one side and kissed me on the mouth. I freed myself, climbed onto the back of the truck, picked up one of the bullhorns, and attempted a speech.

The speech was limp, without conviction. I realized that I didn't really know what "dialectical materialism" meant. And phrases like the state "withering away" or the "dictatorship of the proletariat" were suddenly confusing. Doubts assailed me as I spoke. I regretted that I had been unable to attend school like other people. Any do-it-yourself education, especially one from a poorly stocked library, is bound to have embarrassing gaps.

The librarian, old Mrs. Merkle with the pince-nez, never answered my questions. She only smiled. She probably thought that I could not read. She probably thought it was "cute," the way I took out books and returned them, pretending to be normal. The afflicted are looked upon as children.

The bullhorn, however, was sufficiently loud. And its booming sound revealed my location, thank goodness, to Ramphastidus and his Marxist friends. They appeared in the sky like brilliant kites dipping in the wind, like silent fireworks, red, yellow, and white, descending against the soft magenta of the sunset. A memorable sight. I can still see it.

"You weren't at the bridge," said Ramphastidus, alighting. "Poor organization."

We experienced some difficulty equipping the birds with bullhorns. A toucan's claw is large enough but unaccustomed to holding heavy objects for any length of time. Also, the beak tends to get in the way. But we managed, with straps. Each toucan took a bullhorn and flew off in a different direction, according to Ramphastidus's instructions.

Ramphastidus himself got into position on the roof of the pickup truck and began. He was perfect. If you closed your eyes, you wouldn't have known he was a toucan. A good thing, that the language, whatever the language was, was not for human ears, because the police would have had a fit.

How could people think of partying, asked Ramphastidus, when all around us, in the Colombian countryside, in the streets of Colombian cities, poverty, the worst poverty, was so evident? For this shame he blamed the aristocrats, the plantation owners, the press, the generals, and especially the cocaine tycoons and their lackey politicians. He spoke of fascist dictatorships supported by big business, of decadent jet-setters who squandered the wealth of their nation, and of the Third World's fight everywhere for human dignity. He denounced Washington, the CIA, and the government of Paraguay.

Seeing that this would take time, I went to get a bite to eat. I hadn't had a thing since breakfast. But after more than an hour of elbowing my way through crowds, I realized that no restaurant, no store of any kind, would be open. In any case, all the available food in Barrancabermeja had surely been consumed by now in this raging epidemic of hedonism. I saw people doubled over and vomiting, they had gorged themselves so much.

A giant gray earthworm stuck its reared head out from behind a corner of a building; wet and faceless, it lunged at me, all one hundred feet of it, with the speed of a cannonball. Like a fool, I ducked. A Chivri sang a song about a maiden loath who finally agrees, under pressure, to participate in something unhygienic but enjoyable. A human couple of undetermined sex rolled and slobbered over each other at my feet. Would my idea of using the toucans work? I kept my fingers crossed.

Some revelers, for a joke, tried to push a bus over. Others joined in, laughing. They set it rocking from side to side, more and more. There was a mighty cheer: the bus, at a tilt, was poised to fall. It fell, but fell in the opposite direction and more quickly than was anticipated. I noticed that the gourds in its path, no matter how they were engaged, all hopped nimbly out of the way, so that the only victims were humans. Besotted or befuddled, several people were squashed.

Apparently the Chivris, even in the throes of ecstasy, never lost their presence of mind. In a split second, if the situation required it, they could be completely sober. It annoyed me that they showed such solicitude for their own skins, and that ours didn't matter to them.

Where were the police? Why was there no ambulance? A block farther, I came upon a trampled toucan, its brilliant feathers drab in the dust of the street. A fallen hero. But other bullhorns—I could hear them—persisted, so the cause was not yet lost. The echoed word "duty" hung in the air above me, faint but reproachful.

The partying increased in intensity, became furious. Empty bottles were hurled against walls, and then the people danced wildly on the broken slivers with their bare feet, as if their pain and blood were a practical joke, like having a bucket of water dumped over your head or sitting on a tack. I heard shots: some were whooping it up in the style of cowboys in westerns. One elderly gentleman stood clutching a post in front of a pharmacy; he held a six-gun, but his face was twisted and blue. I guessed that he had been roundly filliped for firing too near a gourd.

"Are you okay?" I asked. His body, half-crouched, was rigid. His lower lip trembled.

I went past him into the pharmacy, with the idea of finding something that might help. I tried the drawers behind the counter, but they were filled with papers, not medicine. I did find Band-Aids and applied a few to my knees, which were badly scraped, although I didn't recall falling down.

Three looters burst in and began shooting—at me. I ducked. This time the reflex was fortunate, because the looters and their bullets were real. I scuttled into a back room on my hands and knees while, laughing, they hurled the cash register to the floor with a tremendous crash.

"Damn! Someone got here before us!" cried one of the men. The cash register, it seemed, was empty.

"The skinny guy!" cried another, meaning me.

"I was only looking for medicine," I called out to them from the back room. "I didn't take any money."

Now, the question was, if they came after me, should I or shouldn't I jump out the window? The window looked onto an alley packed with gourds. If I jumped, I would land on a gourd, and that could be fatal. The looters, on the other hand, looked the type that snuffed out lives easily, for little or no reason.

Out of the corner of my eye I saw something green. An old tarp, cracked and mildewed, lay folded on a chair. Then one of the looters appeared in the doorway, not six feet from me, his gun leveled and a grin on his sweaty face. As the gun went off—I could actually see fire and smoke erupt from the muzzle—I grabbed the tarp, shook it open like a bedsheet, and pulled it over my head and ringing ears as I dove out the window. The gun went bang, bang, bang. It was a miracle I wasn't hit; the looter must have been drunk.

With the tarp I hoped to pass for a gourd, at least at the moment of falling. I hurt my shoulder, but there was no fillip.

"In what do you have faith, brother?" asked a Chivri, pressing against me.

"Fun," I answered, guessing at the catechism. "Pleasure," I tried again, when that met with no success. The Chivri stared at me. I cleared my throat and said, "Making hay while the sun shines." (In Chivri'ese the expression, literally, was "Pinch your sieve unless the fraction.")

We were jostled and separated by a pair of gourds moving through. I took this opportunity to pose the same question to a gourd behind me, to see what the answer was. The answer was: "In nothingness." (Except that in Chivri'ese the word for nothingness had one syllable, not three, and made a sound like a short cough.)

What did it mean, to have faith in nothingness? Was it like having faith in nothing? I heard this exchange again, between two other gourds. It seemed to be a formula of greeting. I pulled the tarp tighter around me and worked my way toward the intersection, where a toucan with a bullhorn was holding forth.

"Together," the toucan said, "we can awaken our nation. Let the cry of the poor be heard throughout the land. From Barranquilla to the Amazon let us rise up as one and cast off the yoke. Together, compadres, we can reaffirm our dignity. We can reach out at last for hope. Our inheritance. Progress. We can modernize. We can stand proud, make the world a better place for our children, for our children's children, and we can purge our shores, once and for all, of the noxious profit motive."

Difficult to pay attention. My shoulder throbbed. The police were present, I saw, but they stood to the side, not interfering. They were amused; they watched. Perhaps they thought that a movie was being filmed.

People fell, but no one helped them up. They were trampled, young and old, completely unnoticed. If they regained their feet, they continued gamely with the party. But many lay still. I saw a gray sailor in the gutter, already stiff with death but smiling horribly out of his bruised face, as if someone had told him a terrific joke at the end.

The gourds churned, danced, made merry with more abandon than ever, as if there were no tomorrow. Several danced with me in a ring. Several invited me to accompany them. In their charades. In their leapfrog. In their copulatory two-step. They copulated upright, avoiding the prone position, perhaps, because of the crowd, which was like Times Square on New Year's Eve.

I saw stars when someone bumped into my shoulder. Under the tarp, I looked at it. A dark stain: blood? Yes, and it went all the way down to my socks. Feeling suddenly weak, I went over to one of the policemen and asked him where the hospital was. He pretended not to understand me. (Was I addressing him in the right language?) A nasty pink bat appeared from behind the policeman's ear and stuck its forked tongue out at me: a taunt.

It was hard work moving through the crowd. Patiently I made for the large stucco building at the end of the street. It turned out to be not a hospital but an empty warehouse. Inside, between some barrels, was a group of small children huddled together and thin as toothpicks. I asked them where the hospital was. They looked at me with enormous eyes. Finally, the oldest child, a girl, informed me that there was a hospital in Bucaramanga. Her sister had had her tonsils removed there and was given Jell-O to eat, as much Jell-O as she liked. Cherry.

"That's too far," I said. I felt feverish. Some gourds, entering the warehouse, invited me to sing with them. I sang, faking the words. In less than a minute my throat was raw (the language had so many impossible velars and glottals), so I had to beg off. Other gourds commenced roughhousing—or playing ball, I wasn't sure—and I was knocked into again, on the bad shoulder. The next thing I knew, I was cramped and half-suffocated in my tarp, under a lot of weight. I must have fainted, and the gourds piled on top of me, as in a football game.

Dizzy, I struggled to my feet. The gourds rolled

off. It had not been any kind of scrimmage, I realized. There was no mistaking the gobs of acrid blue in several places on the tarp. I was—as far as I could tell—untouched myself, intact (except for the shoulder), but I felt humiliated, and wanted nothing more than to be rid of my ridiculous disguise.

The gourds, pursuing another activity, bore me with them out into the street, where I looked for a current in the crowd which would take me away from the town. There were currents going in all directions. Then, by luck, I spotted a sign that read:

BARRANCABERMEJA INFIRMARY
EST. 1823

In the infirmary, an old, bone-white building full of flies and crucifixes, lay people on rows of iron beds. The smell was intolerable. The patients could not get up, and no one had changed them or even emptied the bedpans. My head burned so much, however, that I was tempted to get into one of the beds myself.

"Oh, look, it's a carnival thing!" cried a bloated woman, pointing at me with a feeble hand.

"Excuse me, is there a doctor around?" I asked.

"Everyone's at the carnival," said the woman. "Oh, can we go, too?"

"I'm a human being like yourself." I lifted the tarp to show my face.

She closed her eyes and sank back with a grimace of disappointment.

I went through a courtyard to an office, but the office was deserted. On the desk a speckled bug crawled across an open dictionary. I stopped and considered, with the bug, a long Spanish word that meant division into equal parts.

Why was I standing here? My mind was not functioning; it was the fever. I needed medical attention, probably an antibiotic.

The radio on the desk worked; I got a station—Medellín. Polkas, frantic polkas: suitable accompaniment to the invasion. Then the news came on, crackling. Yes, the gourds had spread as far as Medellín. It didn't seem that the announcer could make up his mind whether or not this was a bad thing. He made mention of the soapbox orators but omitted the fact —or else did not know—that they were not only birds, but leftists.

"The army has been alerted," said the announcer, "but as yet the green mob shows no inclination to violence. Mayor Felice said, in a communiqué issued earlier today, that there is no need to panic and that the whole thing may be only a promotional stunt. The commissioner feels that, considering the numbers involved, this affair could bring in a bit of revenue to Medellín."

I found a doctor in a side room. He was sitting reading a magazine.

"You're not out with the others?" I asked him.

Beetle-browed, he frowned. "I don't like parties," he said, not bothering to look up at me.

"How can you sit there," I was moved to say, "while your patients in the other wing are lying in their filth?"

He turned a page, said nothing, as if I wasn't there.

To hell with the doctor and to hell with the patients, I thought.

The pain in my shoulder was spreading to the arm, neck, and back, taking over the majority of me, so that beside the pain there was little left. I wandered out in search of help. Gourds greeted me.

"In what do you have faith, brother?" one asked.

"In nothingness," I said.

We passed a group of people playing wobbly soccer with an empty whiskey bottle, a group of people convulsed with laughter on the ground, and a group convulsed on the ground erotically. Perhaps having faith in nothingness meant that the Chivris—this species of Öht—believed that in the afterlife there was no gathering of rosebuds, so one had better gather them while one had the chance.

The gourds recruited me for a game that involved climbing up and down a large palm tree in front of a boating-supply store. Rotund, they had great difficulty climbing and at best got two or three feet off the ground; but the difficulty seemed to be the whole point of the game. They put everything they had into it.

Weakened by the shoulder wound, I did worse than any of the gourds, but my trouble pleased them. Cough-coughing in Chivri'ese, they complimented me. My forehead gave out so much heat, it was an oven under the tarp.

Ramphastidus told us to repent of our selfishness. We ignored him, of course. But he was amazingly persistent. What was it, I wondered, that kept do-gooders doing good? All the discouragement they met with, continually, didn't discourage them. I remembered a social worker at Rosedale, Mrs. Evans, who always greeted Frank with a wide, confident smile—as if *today* things would be okay—even though at the first opportunity Frank would try to do away with himself.

If there was nothingness after this existence, a

whole endless sea of nothingness, then it really didn't matter, did it, all this puritanical fuss over right and wrong and what others thought. We passed a beggar thin as a rail. Bent, he stood with one hand out, palm up. More out of habit than hope. Worse luck for you, was my thought. You may starve, but I intend to eat.

I wanted, seeing his bony head and jaw, to sink my teeth into a cheeseburger—into a dozen cheeseburgers—into a hundred cheeseburgers, with millions of french fries.

"How," intoned the toucan, "can you wallow?"

And what was wrong, I thought, with a little wallowing?

"How," intoned the toucan, "can you turn your back on?"

Phooey, I thought, on whatever it is I'm turning my back on. So some have food and some don't. That's Darwin. As long as I don't have to look at it.

We moved away from the bullhorn as one moves away from bad breath.

The problem was, when we got out of its range and wanted to stop to have some fun, the others behind us, still moving, kept us moving, too. All this involuntary moving and shoving grew tedious. I heard a few Believers say that, shit, if this was the way it was here, they would go someplace else. The thought of wasting valuable time like this was indeed exasperating. Sacrilegious.

And the police just grinned like imbeciles.

So we hurried back to the porthole, followed by the boring bullhorns (who couldn't even speak the language right, the ridiculous way they drew out their *hgkg's* to two or three syllables). We were filled with contempt for the natives, whose notions of a good time were primitive, to say the least. We were fed up

strange novelty. Ejaculating gave no relief. I went downstairs to find some rum, to help me get to sleep, but none of the bars in the hotel were open.

On the plane home, drinks were available, but they tasted vile. This, I stopped to think, was my first acquaintance with alcohol. I also smoked—also for the first time. The cigarettes made me light-headed. I pictured myself, a drink in one hand and a cigarette in the other, and thought, chuckling, that Lucille would not recognize me now. I told jokes to the people across the aisle from me, but they stuck their faces in their magazines and pretended not to hear.

No reporters greeted me at the airport with flash cameras; no official from the State Department came forward to debrief me; no one even shook my hand and said thanks. I wondered how Ramphastidus was doing, in his forest, and whether Mr. Vélez was back with his textiles. I had fried shrimp for supper, at a restaurant, then a steak, then ham. The waitress stared. My hands shook.

Four brown zombies sprang up out of my front lawn as I opened the gate. In a chorus line they sang, "Car-pay-dee-em, car-pay-dee-em," then vanished, leaving only their stink in the air.

Home sweet home, I thought.

I called Lucille. She wasn't in. I went out again and bought a big bottle of whiskey. Without alcohol I would be up all night ejaculating. But instead of knocking me out, the whiskey made me wild. I broke glasses on the kitchen floor, turned on the sprinkler in the back (with the stars looking down), and then, wearing nothing but my sling, called Lucille at three in the morning and made an indecent proposal. Then I ran outside for a while and let dogs bark at me.

At one point I said to myself, seriously, that I

must shampoo the living room rug to get rid of the red footprints. The rug wasn't mine, it belonged to old Mr. Forbes. Old Mr. Forbes didn't like messes.

I raided the icebox and ate the rest of the potatoes, just as they were from the sack—skin, dirt, eyes, and all—and, puffing like a steam engine, copulated with the rough and dusty sofa.

The next thing I knew, it was morning, and the singing of the birds was such torture to me that I wished, I honestly wished, that I was dead.

On to Omsk

The next Öht were almost the opposite of the Chivri. They looked like macramé, extremely dry, and they came not in search of pleasure but in search of novelty, being bored. Also, there were only a few of them, relatively. No more than two or three hundred. I learned of their impending invasion from a candy wrapper (clever Conservationists!). The small print was laconic: OMSK, OCT 20, 2 P.M. I had, this time, a month to prepare.

No airplane ticket arrived in the mail, and I decided that I had better not wait for one. If time ran out, and a ticket didn't materialize at the last minute, I would be on the wrong side of the globe when the Öht struck, and my peripheral, handy as it had shown itself to be, would not be able to bail me out of *that* predicament. So I booked a flight, round-trip, and paid out of my own pocket.

Lucille, when I told her about the message on the candy wrapper, reminded me that I needed a visa and that the Soviet Union's wheels of bureaucracy, as a rule, turned slowly and unreliably.

Therefore I had better apply at their consulate right away.

The consulate, near the United Nations, was in a modern office building that had no hint of Mother Russia. The secretaries were normal women, not built like wrestlers, and they didn't wear babushkas or boots. One, leaning back, filed her fingernails quietly with an emery board. When she spoke to tell me what forms I was supposed to fill out, she had hardly any accent.

My destination interested her. Very few people, she said, went to Omsk. I had relatives there, yes?

I shook my head.

"You are on business, then?" inquired the secretary.

"I'm in textiles."

"How interesting. Yes, Omsk is known for its manufacture of textiles. What American company do you represent?"

Omsk, like Barrancabermeja, was an industrial town located on a river. (But, then, most industrial towns in the world are located on rivers, since rivers provide power as well as a way to dispose of wastes. Omsk also, like Barrancabermeja, possessed a large oil refinery. Could it be that oil refineries somehow drew the Öht?)

"It's a small company," I said, my face hot. "You wouldn't have heard of it."

A bright green earthworm came toward me menacingly across the desk. I averted my eyes.

"Do you speak Russian?" asked the secretary.

"That won't be a problem."

She looked at me questioningly. Then I understood that she needed to know whether or not their

government, through Intourist, would have to supply
me with a translator on my business trip.

My peripheral allowed me to say a few sentences,
to show her. She made a fuss about how well I spoke.
"You *must* be of Russian extraction! Your parents?"

Embarrassed, I changed the subject. My parents,
as far as I knew—at least according to Aunt Penny—
belonged to a screwball commune on the West Coast
where people went around in white robes and didn't
believe in children.

I do not have an image of my parents, beyond
the fact that my father was tall and wore a mustache.

No problem with the visa. The secretary stamped
a paper and handed it to me with a smile.

Mr. Tribovich, when I told him I was leaving for
Russia and therefore couldn't put lime down for the
winter as he suggested (the subject was grass and acid-
ity), became instantly serious. He waved me over. I
approached the fence between us. With a large stained
hand he gripped my shoulder and pulled me even
nearer, as if there were agents of the KGB in both
our backyards, behind the bushes, straining their ears
to catch American conversation.

"Wally," he said in a gravelly voice, "don't trust 'em.
They lie, they lie all the time. That's all they know."

I began to reply that the Russians, I thought, were
probably people like everybody else, but he shook his
head. He leaned over and brought his lips so close
that for a moment it seemed that he was going to
plant a kiss on my cheek. He whispered, "My brother-
in-law."

Mr. Tribovich was a Croat, but his sister had married a Russian. He said "Russian" as if Russian were
reptilian. He knew from personal experience.

I promised I would keep my guard up.

At the airport, Bea handed me a present: a pair of earmuffs. "It's probably below zero there," she said, explaining the practicality of it to cover her confusion.

"But it won't even be winter there," I protested.

"It's *Siberia,* for heaven's sake."

I accepted the present and thanked her as graciously as I could. She was after me; it was painfully obvious. Misfits, somehow, seek each other out— when it makes the most sense for them to hook up with people who are normal. Bea wasn't from Rosedale but had been put away for a while in a place upstate, as a result of some family trauma. She was young, poor thing, not even twenty-one.

A chasm opened up in the ground as I walked with the other passengers to the plane. It took me by surprise. I actually flinched and stumbled, as in the old days. "Wally," I told myself, "get your mind off women."

On the way to Omsk, from Moscow, there were several stops, all at towns that ended with *sk.* Sverdlovsk. Chelyabinsk. Tobolsk. Tyukalinsk. Our small, single-engine plane shook like an old bus, reminding me of my nauseating, daylong ride, not that long ago, from Bucaramanga to Barrancabermeja.

I wondered what Ramphastidus would think, to be in the stronghold, as it were, of Marxism. The toucan would need a sweater.

The pilot said nothing. He smoked foul-sweet Bulgarian cigarettes, one after the other, and sipped tea out of a discolored plastic mug. When the plane lurched, which was often, the tea spilled. Each time, the pilot carefully refilled his mug from a thermos. He spent more time with the tea than with the controls.

I never saw a grayer landscape. It was like being in the middle of an old newsreel—from the thirties or forties—where even the children and the flowers seemed to have dinge on them.

"Smoke and tea," I said to the pilot, "will stain your teeth."

He turned slowly to me and winked. "I'm an old married man. It doesn't matter if my teeth are brown."

A woman whose destination was farther than mine, Irkutsk, and who had been complaining all day about shortages, told us that her sister in Tomsk once made seven hundred rubles profit in a week selling tubes of toothpaste that she bought by the carton in Moscow, because in Tomsk toothpaste couldn't be had for love or money after the Christmas season. People used either baking soda or salt.

Another passenger, a man with a tuft of hair at the bottom of his chin, said that in Tomsk there used to be a dentist who gave his lady patients gas so that he could feel them up.

The woman whose destination was Irkutsk replied, raising her voice, that the best remedy she knew for toothache was a poultice that contained mint and camphor, which her mother, God rest her soul, used during the war, when they didn't have the luxury of such things as dentists.

Then the plane took a dip and everyone held on. The pilot lit another cigarette. Bulgarian smoke hung in the air as we dipped and dipped. Were the passengers as ill as I was? Their pinched, weather-beaten faces showed no greenness. These were people accustomed to discomfort.

Finally we landed. Lugging my suitcase, I walked around for a while, to get my bearings. The point of entry for the invasion, I figured, would be the town's only landmark, the statue at the central square: an ugly, high, huge bronze representation of a group of citizens marching, their heads raised as if listening to some celestial announcement. Instead of banners or swords they carried shovels and hoes.

After supper, in my room at the hotel, the Komsomolyetz, I discovered that I had fleas. The bites were painful and itched. Cursing, I went to the drugstore around the corner, but the pharmacist, a man with a round head and hardly any hair, told me with an idiotic grin that there was no such thing as a poison for fleas.

"Then what do you people do," I asked angrily, "if your dogs have fleas?"

The pharmacist grinned even wider. (Perhaps in Omsk dogs were not kept as pets. Or perhaps the natives here would not dream of putting anything on themselves that was used for their dogs. I reminded myself that I was in a foreign country.)

I tried taking a bath. The rusty water that trickled from the spigot in the tub was cold, no matter which knob I turned. I splashed rubbing alcohol on myself, to discourage the fleas. Shivering, I wrapped a blanket around me, but found that the blanket too was infested with fleas. This was a hundred times worse than the hot night and the mosquitoes in Barrancabermeja. I didn't sleep a wink.

The hallucinations, too, were more troublesome than usual, possibly on account of jet lag. Lucille appeared at one point. Her hair was green with streaks of white, and when she opened her mouth, the flicking forked tongue of a snake emerged diabolically. It was the first time I had ever seen Lucille in a hallucination. I wondered what, if anything, that signified.

In the morning I took two pills instead of one, and an aspirin for the flea bites. After a glass of hot tea and a little black bread and herring, I began to feel human. I went for a walk. The air was invigorating but had the sour smell of factories. Was there no place free of pollution? A street with potholes followed the curve of the river. The slate-gray river, the Om, seemed motionless beneath the heavy sky. On a barge out in the middle of the water a man sat on a chair and scrubbed a boot that he held in his hand. The scrub-scrub-scrub was as regular as sawing.

"Welcome to Omsk," said a voice. A man came toward me, smiling, from one of the bridges. He looked very Russian: fur hat, a thick, black beard. "Allow me to introduce myself," he said, showing his teeth. "My name is Anatoly—" I didn't catch the last name. Sergeyevich? We shook hands.

"I suppose it's obvious that I'm a visitor," I said.

He laughed. "It's obvious. And you come from the United States, even though you speak flawlessly."

"My clothes."

"Actually, it's more in the way a person carries himself. How he holds his head, what he does with his hands." Anatoly demonstrated. "A Frenchman is relaxed, unselfconscious. He moves his head around easily. The German is stiffer in the spine and neck, and his hands hang at his side or else they are carrying something. He never loiters."

"And Italians gesticulate," I suggested.

"Italians walk unafraid, with their bellies out."

Anatoly accompanied me on my stroll along the river. Before I knew it, I was calling him Tolya and he was calling me Wally—except that, in Russian, Wally sounded like "volley," as in volleyball. I asked

him what to do about fleas. He told me to use oil—
cooking oil. "One smells like a salad," he said. "But
there are worse things to smell like."

Tolya worked as an engineer of some kind, but
the passion of his life was ballet. He had a collection
of records, a collection of books, and a collection of
autographed portraits of world-famous dancers. He
pirouetted and leaped as he spoke, not constrained
by his hat or coat. "But Moscow is so far," he sighed.
"You have no idea what it's like, Volley, living out
here in the middle of nowhere. The last ballet troupe
that came to Omsk—it was more than a year ago—
and, ah, they were dreadful."

I commiserated. I knew a New Yorker (John,
who did inventory at my department store) who had
suffered similar ennui when visiting his aunt in Minnesota.

Tolya invited me to his apartment to see the
autograph of the great Bondaryov. "Let us keep our
fingers crossed," he said to me, "that they don't let
him out of the country. Our great dancers all defect
to the West. And then, you know, I would never
see Bondaryov again, even if I went to Moscow,
which, believe me, I can't afford to do often." We
turned down a side street of flagstones and white-
washed walls. The wind played with a few withered
leaves; they spiraled in the corners, rising and falling
slowly.

The apartment was in a large, modern building
that stood unconnected to any road or sidewalk. You
reached it by going through a courtyard and around
a field of rubble. "Construction," Tolya explained.
The concrete of the facade had cracks and patches
everywhere, and rust stains fell like waterfalls of
brown from the railings on all the balconies, floor after

floor. Over the entrance a long, bright red-and-white banner announced:

50 YEARS OF THE UNION OF METALLURGY PRODUCTION
"CAUCASUS"

Inside, we climbed several flights of stairs. I was introduced to a fat woman named Irena Matvyeyevna Syeryebryakina and her female cousin, shorter, with a sunny smile, whose name was Dorotyeya Vassilyevna Shchebotinskaya. Tolya's father, Sergey, sat at the kitchen table and waved lazily: no need for formalities. I never learned what relationship Irena Matvyeyevna and her cousin were to Tolya, but they seemed to take the place of his mother, whose photograph stood framed in silver on the dresser. They fussed over inconsequential things the way mothers fuss, and everyone, the father included, deferred to them. A thin man with a sardonic smile shook my hand. An athletic younger woman asked me, poking her face into mine, what I thought about dolphins being murdered by the Japanese for cat food.

The autographs were in an old trunk under Tolya's bed. "My riches," he said to me, winking, but it was clear that he meant it. He showed me, silently, the picture of the great Bondaryov: a blond, clean-shaven man in profile, a halo of diffused light, an outstretched hand, an open chest, and a large, ornate belt around a narrow waist.

Dorotyeya Vassilyevna insisted that I have tea. While I sipped, she questioned me closely, as if I had come to seek her daughter's hand in marriage. She introduced me to a family that said not a word the whole time but huddled together and grinned incessantly.

"This is life in Omsk," the younger, athletic woman said. "You'll have to excuse us."

Irena Matvyeyevna, looming, objected. "Nonsense, Yevdoxia Fyodorovna. There are many fine people here."

"As a Communist," said a dour, sandy-haired teenager, who had terrible acne, "I find nothing wrong with Omsk."

Tolya burst into laughter. He took me by the arm and, before anyone could protest, bore me out. "I saw him once," he said as we went quickly down the stairs, our footsteps making echoes. "He was window-shopping on Volga Street, in Moscow, dressed like you or me. But such grace! Such presence!"

"The young Communist?"

"What? No, *Bondaryov!*" Tolya stopped, his mouth open. "My God, what a thought!" He shook his head. "No, the mind refuses to consider such a thing!"

"Consider what?"

"That Arkady Bondaryov ever could have had a problem, even momentarily, with his complexion."

"Tolya, you're a romantic."

"Volley, it's true, I am. Hopelessly."

We had lunch in a small, stand-up eating place called The Gastronome. My hot dog disagreed with me: too much garlic, and there were pieces of bone and gristle in it. Then I saw steaming feces on my plate, and that didn't help. Tolya said it would take time for the stomach to adjust. The culture of the East was so unlike the culture of the West, culinarily.

He tried to take my mind off my indigestion by showing me around the Omsk "Cossack" Sawmill, in whose yards and barns, he claimed, lived some of the world's largest spiders. "Climb onto the logs and

stamp your feet. You'll see them. They run like mad."
He made rapid wriggling motions with the fingers of
both hands. We climbed and stamped, but nothing
happened, except that a guard approached and told
us to get the hell off the wood.

The sweet smell of the wood at the sawmill reminded me of home and the time I had tried, with a
couple of friends, to build a tree house for the winter.
I think we even planned to have a stove installed. The
idea was to be snowed in from Halloween to Easter
and not have to go to school, and so on. It struck me
odd, suddenly, that I was now an adult.

"Are you well?" Tolya asked.

"I'm coming down with something." My head
throbbed. I thanked him, excused myself, and returned to the Komsomolyetz, where the murderous
fleas waited. The only oil that the management could
find for me was a bottle of peppermint oil, and the
smell was overwhelming. I gritted my teeth and
rubbed the stuff on myself, all over, before climbing
into bed, as if it was insect repellent and I was in a
tent in the woods. The fumes were so powerful that
even when I burped garlic, the peppermint masked
it completely. I dreamt that I was being pursued by
candy canes.

"What have I done to you?" I gasped, in my
dream.

"Nothing," they said, pursuing. "We want to give
you acne."

Bully for Psylla

The alarm clock went off, three days later, with a jarring buzz. I was getting over the flu, feeling stronger. I was also becoming accustomed to the bites (the fleas didn't mind the oil, of course) and accustomed to the dismal Soviet excuse for a toilet down the hall. Apparently, one could live even in Omsk. But the alarm clock bothered me; there was something not right about it.

What was not right about it was that I did not have an alarm clock. Immediately I suspected the Conservationists. Was the invasion beginning? I jumped out of bed, pulled on my pants.

"But wait," I cried, "it's not the twentieth yet." It was only October the seventeenth.

The alarm buzzed even louder, as if to say that the date (idiot!) didn't matter. What if these particular Öht were dropping in early, ahead of schedule? I grabbed my coat and ran out, down the stairs, into the street, as fast as my legs could carry me. A minute, I well knew, might make all the difference.

There was nothing at the bronze collective-farm

statue in the main square. Where, then, was the landing site? I hurried back, toward the river. Nothing on the river. I ran to the refinery, remembering the last invasion and wondering if there would be, near the refinery, a cemetery on a hill overlooking the river—although such a repetition of circumstances seemed farfetched, inasmuch as the different races of Öht were unrelated (so said the Conservationists) even by planet of origin.

A cluster of chemical tanks, cranes, and smoke-stacks stood where the two rivers came together, the Om and the Irtysh. It brought to mind Pittsburgh. No hill in sight, no graveyard. Heated from the running, I unzipped my coat and stopped to catch my breath. My breath made clouds in the air, and I noticed that a few tiny flakes were falling. Winter started much sooner here than in New Jersey. Bea was right.

Refuse floated in the water, clumps of straw. A miserable place to live, I thought. Couldn't the enemy from outer space have selected a more scenic spot to invade? The pieces of straw, bobbing, collected by the edge of the quay, then lifted slowly into the air, not wet at all, somehow, but dry, like mats forgotten in a dusty attic for a hundred years. Uh-oh, I said to myself, this is it.

The straw clumps, rising along the concrete of the quay, assumed a vertical position as they rose. They were more like hanging nets, now, than clumps of straw, or, rather, like hangings of macramé. They floated up to my level, each suspended about two feet above the ground, which gave them an overall height of at least eight feet. The height contributed to their aura of superiority. I cleared my throat.

"What can I do for you?" I asked, surprised at how sibilant the language was.

"What do you have here that's different?" whistled the macramé closest to me.

"Different from what?"

The macramé made a wry sound. "Well answered. I could not have answered better." Then it seemed to wait for me to continue.

To say something, I asked it the name of its race. It made a side-to-side motion, in the negative, which meant (I guessed) that the question was inappropriate or irrelevant. I asked it its individual name, giving my own, as if we were being introduced at some social function. Again, it shook its head (figuratively speaking, of course, since there was no head as such).

It took notice of a pigeon flying past.

"That's a pigeon," I said, wishing I knew more about pigeons. "They eat corn, pieces of bread, almost anything; they roost on buildings, in cities."

"Do you have a brochure?" asked the macramé.

I looked at it blankly. A brochure on pigeons?

The macramé sighed. "I suppose we will have to fend for ourselves. Any suggestions?"

"You mean—things to see?" Now I understood: these were tourists and they required an itinerary. Well, what did Earth have to offer? I tried to think. "There's a Mount Rushmore with faces carved in the side. Not on this continent, but . . ."

"On Tikafa Two," whistled the macramé wearily, "there is a mountain chain hundreds of thousands of miles in length, and it is sculpted in the precise image of a recumbent female of the Vor species. Vor pilots can see it, when the clouds do not intervene, from half a million miles out in space, with the naked eye."

"Not to mention Yv, and Solog B," hissed another macramé that looked like a matted mop. "And, of course, Moofnakorb." Several macramés nodded dejectedly.

I was about to say that we had a Grand Canyon, but realized that the response would be the same. If these people had been all over the galaxy, no wonder of *our* world, man-made or natural, could possibly spark their interest. They were bound to have seen something like it before, and probably more so, and probably many times over. I sympathized with them.

"Perhaps," suggested the first macramé, though without much hope, "your natives have peculiar customs."

"Perhaps," said the matted mop, "there is some incredible coincidence in your history."

I shook my head, and they shook their heads (figuratively) with me. Then a voice piped up, in my mind: "Whose side are you *on*, Wally? Don't you want these Öht to go *away*? Wasn't *that* the idea?" I answered mentally: "Of course. You're absolutely right."

"I'm afraid," I said to the aliens, "that Earth is a very boring planet."

There was an awkward pause.

"Interesting," whistled the macramé. "The soft sell."

"I don't think anyone's tried that on us before," observed one of the other macramés, obviously younger.

"Oh, they have," said another macramé, a dishwater shade. "On Bleegee, on New Chiz. But it doesn't happen often. Local pride, most places."

Meanwhile, some Russians had gathered and were staring. An elderly woman crossed herself; her lips moved. Would we have trouble with the police? But I was coming to the conclusion that the police, in every country, exercised limited vision where tourists were concerned. Foreigners did not lie in their jurisdiction.

I found that I was relaxed. These Öht certainly did not seem dangerous; they spoke intelligently, and if their attitude was somewhat negative, it was in no way—as far as I could see—fanatical, violent, or disruptive of the fabric of human civilization. What harm would there be if they nosed about?

But the voice inside me fussed. "What *harm*? You're *already* under their spell, Wally, and not even *fighting* it."

"Gentlemen," I addressed the macramés, "I think that whoever referred you to us made a mistake; there's really nothing to see here, but you're welcome to have a look for yourselves."

"Curious," whistled the first macramé. "We are accustomed to posters and promises."

"They may have something unusual," whispered the matted mop. "I doubt it, but they just may."

The aliens drifted off slowly in different directions, presumably to investigate. It was odd, I thought, the way the people followed them. Younger children sometimes follow older children in that silent, big-eyed, submissive manner. The macramés were, indeed, impressive, and not merely in appearance. You sensed that each glum, drab tangle of string had been around for a millennium at least. Any opinion from an entity like that carried weight.

I watched. A macramé floated over to an object —a lamppost, a sign, a doorway—and inspected it as the people crowded around; it sighed and moved on, and the people followed. The same sigh was accorded to everything, big or small, old or new, expensive or inexpensive, animal, vegetable, or mineral.

The aliens' weariness had no difficulty crossing the language barrier. I saw one man, big-bellied and red in the face, lug a silver samovar from his home: his prize possession. The macramé paused, considered the object briefly from its height of eight feet, sighed, and continued on. The man dropped the samovar and joined the group, leaving the shining heirloom on its side, in the street, with a dent.

Tour guides, I thought, were needed. There was so much the macramés could not appreciate without an explanation. Perhaps, employing the peripheral, I could arrange something along the lines of what was done in Barrancabermeja. There were no toucans to recruit in Omsk, of course, but . . . "You see?" said the voice, interrupting again. "You're considering ways to assist the Öht instead of *discouraging* them. Ramphastidus? He drove them *out*—he certainly didn't cheer them *on*!"

Where had I picked up this conscience? Was it a Conservationist plant? For a conscience, the voice hardly qualified as "still" or "small"; it set my teeth on edge, like the sound of a fingernail across a dry blackboard. But it had a point. My duty was to stem the invasions, not facilitate them. I tried to get my brain working.

Drowsiness made it hard for me to concentrate. The snowflakes, sinking vertically and silently through the air, had a soporific effect. Did it really matter, did it really hurt so much if we were visited by a group of scraggly sight-seeing mats from another planet?

Well, what would get rid of them? Thinking, I returned to the hotel for some breakfast. The food was the same, depressing. Whatever the Russians ate, it seemed, was either greasy, sour, smoked, or stale.

I went up to my room, lay in bed, burped foully, and stared at the ceiling. Little wonder, I thought, that alcoholism was a problem in this part of the world. There was no character in the land or sky, nothing to focus on. Featureless fields. Anonymous houses. Everything bleak and overcast.

I dozed until twelve, was awakened by a sharp bite on my shoulder. I caught the offender between thumb and forefinger. "Damn you," I said. "If you were bigger—" I wanted to take the creature by the neck and throttle it.

"If I were bigger," said the flea, "I wouldn't be a flea."

"What are you speaking, flea-ese?"

"Size," it replied, "shouldn't make anybody patronizing."

"I'm tired of being bitten."

"I have to make a living," said the flea. "Do you think I enjoy spending hours in people's armpits?"

"I'm sorry, I have no sympathy for parasites."

"Everybody is a parasite."

It was bad enough getting into a conversation with vermin. Now I had to listen to vermin philosophy. The flea, given the chance, would no doubt argue that we humans did away with cows to provide ourselves with hamburgers, whereas noble fleadom, revering life, left its hosts in one piece, etc. I looked around for a match or hard objects I could use to crush the thing between. There was a heavy glass ashtray—and, in my pocket, the room key.

But, as I leaned over to put the villain in the ashtray, I received another bite—on the hip—that caused me to release my grip. The flea, difficult enough to see when imprisoned in my hand, squirmed, jumped, and immediately was out of sight. I cursed. "You have an accomplice."

"My brother," called the flea from somewhere near the headboard. "His name is Pulex."

"Now that you've dined off me, we can introduce ourselves, is that it?"

"Normally we don't speak to people. They can't understand us," answered the flea. "And they probably wouldn't talk to us, anyway, if they could. My name is Siphon."

"I'm sure you come from a large family."

"All that is left of us, besides Pulex and me, is a younger sister. Her name is Psylla. We haven't seen Psylla in months, but we understand she's married."

"Bully for Psylla," I said. "That's just wonderful. More fleas to puncture me in the night."

"No need to make such a big deal out of it," said Siphon. "The red spots go away after a day or two."

"It's not personal," Pulex spoke up from the foot of the bed. "We're only following our natures. Fulfilling our biological destiny, as a great flea once said."

"I would think you'd be bored stiff," I said in his direction, "doing the same thing generation after generation."

"Fleas, being small," answered Pulex, who sounded like a scholar (I imagined him wearing thick glasses), "are too immersed in detail, in the minutiae of life, to suffer boredom."

"You see things up close," I said.

"We have no other way to see them."

In the flea's-eye view (as opposed to the bird's-eye view), where the horizon would be little more than a millimeter away, the least object, blocking out all others at a given moment, would have importance.

Therefore a flea would not know the meaning of the word "insignificant" or "trivial," or even "typical." It seemed to me (the wheels turning in my head) that Siphon and Pulex would make good tour guides for the macramés.

I explained the situation and asked them if they would like to help. "You will be able to point out things to the macramés," I said, "that no one else would notice." (My conscience started kicking again, but I turned a deaf ear to it. One thing at a time, I said to myself.) My peripheral, I told Siphon and Pulex, would have no difficulty setting up the necessary macramese-flea-ese link to make communication possible. And they could ride on the macramés themselves.

"Bring your nephews and nieces," I said. "We'll need a few hundred, I think."

"Would you object to lice?" asked Siphon.

"Lice?" (Lice also spoke? But why shouldn't they?)

"I have a lot of friends who are lice. They see things that even fleas miss, and they have a quaint sense of humor."

"The same language?"

"We manage. We're thrown together a bit."

I could picture a group of minute beings holding a conference in my scalp. The thought made me extremely itchy.

Pulex raised the question of food. The macramés would probably "offer no sustenance." I told him that each macramé was being followed by a number of human spectators. The fleas and lice ought to be able to tank up whenever they needed, by hopping on and off.

The brothers retreated a little, put their heads together (I had the impression), and, whispering, discussed my proposal. Then Siphon reappeared on my arm—I could actually see him, though there wasn't very much to see. "Not to sound mercenary," he said. "But you have to understand, we fleas live mostly hand-to-mouth. It's a tough world. If we do this thing you want, what's in it for us?"

I didn't have a ready answer. "Well, I suppose, if the macramés are really the menace they're supposed to be—according to the Conservationists— though I don't see how, then the whole human race could theoretically be wiped out. I know it seems unlikely. I *was* shown some pretty frightening pictures."

"Fleas can manage, you realize," said Siphon, "without people."

There were other animals, he meant.

"Of course, then we would have to compete," Pulex pointed out to his brother, "with other species of flea better adapted to hosts of the four-legged variety."

"What could I offer you in payment?" I asked, having no idea.

"There's a soap and a smoke," said Siphon after some thought, "that the people here use against us. Nasty stuff."

I promised that I would see what I could do about the curtailment of the use of the soap and the smoke. The deal was struck. We shook hands, figuratively.

My Russian fur hat, I decided, would be the means of taxiing them and their cousins to their various stations. "All aboard," I cried, throwing on my coat. "And please confine yourselves to the hat." I jogged back to the stone quay across from the refinery, figuring that the macramés, even if they spread, would not travel fast. And, in fact, it took me only an hour, running in and out of different streets, to catch up with all the aliens and discharge my invisible passengers. Under my breath I wished them luck.

The voice inside my head observed sourly that the only thing that would keep me from going down in history as the world's greatest traitor would be that in a year (or however long the annihilation took) there wouldn't *be* any history.

"I'm doing my best," I said.

"For whom?" sneered the voice.

It was true that if the fleas proved successful as tour guides, the macramés would have more reason to stay, and the longer the macramés stayed, the greater the peril to us, etc. It was true, logical, but somehow unconvincing. "Perhaps the important thing," I thought, "is not to combat the Öht, in this particular case, but to combat their attitude."

Warm from my exercise, and hungry, I looked for a restaurant. Surely there was a better place to eat than the Komsomolyetz. Near a garage I found a small place that served borscht. Old people, wearing their coats and hats even though it was hot inside, stood along a counter and slurped methodically, bent over their bowls. The window was completely steamed up, as in the public showers of a gym or swimming pool.

Disappointingly, the borscht turned out to be watery. The bread had no taste at all. Ashes. What a dreary, difficult existence these people led. All their country's money went into missiles, so the food was bad. Donald Duck stuck his head out of the borscht, but I ignored him.

The back of my head itched, around the ears. Had some of the cursed vermin chosen to remain on me? Did I hear a faint tittering, in louse language, behind me? Setting my jaw, I went to the pharmacy by the hotel and bought a bar of medicinal soap. But then, leaving, I remembered my promise to Si-phon. I went back, took some large bills out of my wallet, and bought the pharmacist's entire stock of the soap, which was three cartons. The bald pharmacist grinned, but I didn't care.

I inquired how to make the fumigating smoke. He said that the fumes from hickory, pine tar, and herbs combined sometimes helped. For the herbs I would have to go to the market. This store, that store; this street, that street. I trudged through the snow. After a good deal of trudging through the snow, and parting with more than half my rubles to buy the fumigating herbs, I felt that I had done my part to clean Omsk out of its aids against lice and fleas. I dumped the cartons and packages in the river when no one was looking, but held on to my one bar of soap: for those of Psylla's ilk who hadn't kept their part of the bargain. "No free meals," I muttered. "Not on me."

On the way to my room, the manager beckoned. I had received a postcard from the United States of America. A picturesque scene of a horse farm in Mon-mouth County. From Bea. Her writing was extremely small and cramped, expressing her timidity. I knew that Bea wished to write me a whole letter but hadn't dared.

With the sour-smelling medicinal suds in my hair and the tap going drip-drip-drip, I sat in the barely lukewarm tub (trying not to shiver) and read the post-card.

"Wally," Bea wrote, "I hope you're having a good time in the Soviet Union. Don't get frostbite. Are the earmuffs comfortable? Nothing much is new around here. I'm trying to teach myself how to touch-type. I have to build up my pinkies. Know any exercises? Well, I'm sure you'll have loads of stories to tell when you get back. Watch out for the vodka. Yours, Bea."

"The soap won't work," remarked a tiny voice, "unless you use it three times a day, for a week."

"Thank you for the information," I said darkly. I didn't think I could endure the smell for an entire week.

"And then," continued the louse, "you have to comb the nits out with a fine-tooth comb."

"Why are you telling me all this? Don't you want to survive?"

The louse sighed, fading. "We can't help but survive."

What did that mean? Perhaps, as Siphon suggested, there was something really different about lice.

I felt bad that I had completely forgotten about the earmuffs. Not that I ever wore earmuffs. The least I could do, to be polite, was try them on. However, when I got out of the tub and dried off, I couldn't find them. They weren't in the suitcase, drawer, or closet.

Ho Hum

What sort of tour guides did the fleas make? They
were not discouraged easily.

I went to see how Siphon was faring and heard
the following exchange in a shoe-repair shop on Grokhovoy Street. The shoemaker stared, unable to per-
ceive either language, while a group of twenty people
stood waiting patiently. Siphon's macramé was a dun
color and hung heavier than most.

SIPHON: . . . last year, on that old calendar on the
wall, a fly was swatted, and was squashed dead-center
in the square that happened to be the owner's birth-
day, August 2. You can see the brown spot. The
owner, Arkady Mikhailovich, hasn't torn off the
month-sheets since, or replaced the calendar, out of
superstition. He believes in omens.

MACRAMÉ: If that is meant to amuse, I've heard
a hundred anecdotes, all true, that are far more re-
markable and worlds funnier. On Qloh Three, for
example, an autochthon—

SIPHON: Arkady Mikhailovich is Omsk's tallest shoemaker. He stands, in his stocking feet, 1.8 meters.

MACRAMÉ: There is a shoemaker on Girre, in the town of Sturwid-by-the-Brook, who has five legs and stands, hatless, 19.6 meters. His name escapes me.

SIPHON: At that height, if he tripped and fell, he would die.

MACRAMÉ: No, the gravity is less there.

I found Pulex in the company of two macramés (and about two dozen human spectators) in a vacant lot facing the apartment building in which Tolya lived. One could make out, squinting, the red-and-white banner that said:

50 YEARS OF THE UNION OF METALLURGY PRODUCTION
"CAUCASUS"

Pulex was telling the macramés about local weeds.

PULEX: You can't see much now, because of the season, but we get several varieties of Queen Anne's lace here. It is believed that this ubiquitous Eurasian plant is the source of the cultivated carrot. You would never guess that fact from its roots, however, which are quite bitter.

MACRAMÉ 1: What is a carrot?

PULEX: A carrot is a large, orange, edible root that people put in soups. Rabbits also like it.

MACRAMÉ 1: What are rabbits?

MACRAMÉ 2: I do not find any of this interesting.

MACRAMÉ 1: We may hit on something.

MACRAMÉ 2: I doubt it.

PULEX: A rabbit is a mammal with long ears. It twitches its nose and likes carrots.

MACRAMÉ 2: On Zir there is an animal called the bahezan; it has a tapered tail and eats the green fruit of the fôf tree.

PULEX: What is the point you are making?

MACRAMÉ 2: That there is no point—just as there is no point to your carrots and your rabbits.

Farther on, at an intersection, a louse was directing its macramé to a movie theater, the Volga, an old building of peeling white brick. The film playing, according to the poster in front, was *Brothers of the Steppe*.

LOUSE: If you will come this way . . .

MACRAMÉ: An entertainment area?

LOUSE: The Volga seats three hundred people.

MACRAMÉ: On Chamzifa'ulbzi, I saw an auditorium that held a million. There were twenty tiers. Not a chair empty.

LOUSE: This is only Omsk.

MACRAMÉ: And less than a light-year away, on New Chiss, or New Fiss—doesn't matter—they have an opera house where the cast typically numbers in the tens of thousands, while the audience consists of one person.

LOUSE: Omsk has two movie theaters. The name of the other theater, on Red Star Street, is The Young Guard.

MACRAMÉ: (sighs)

LOUSE: You will see, as you enter, on the right, a mural depicting Lenin addressing the masses at the Winter Palace. The artist, a native of Omsk—

MACRAMÉ: (makes a sound analogous to a stifled yawn)

LOUSE:—Ivan Grigoriyev, passed away only last

week at the age of eighty-nine. His son, Fyodor, collects sticks of chewing gum from all over the world. Fyodor Ivanovich developed an interest in this hobby from attending the movies at the Volga while his father worked. The young people of the town like to chew gum at the movies. At home, you see, most parents disapprove, partly because it is believed that it is not good for the teeth, but partly, also, because chewing gum is relatively rare in the Soviet Union and therefore relatively expensive. The lighting is dim, but stuck to the underside of these seats you will find—

I checked back on Siphon. The flea had taken its macramé to a laundry. Large, broad women stood holding bundles of clothes, their mouths open. The dun macramé was obliged to stoop, being too high for the wrapped pipes that ran in all directions along the ceiling. But Siphon was calling its attention to an object on the floor.

SIPHON: Near the radiator, on that tile, by the wall, is a small crack. Do you see it?

MACRAMÉ: Um.

SIPHON: Inside that crack lives a creature so small that I am to it as you are to me.

MACRAMÉ: On the world of Alabla there are beings as minute as germs.

SIPHON: This creature is a chess master.

MACRAMÉ: Chess masters, in the universe, are as numerous as sand.

SIPHON: It can predict whole games in the blink of an eye.

MACRAMÉ: I am sorry for it.

SIPHON: Why sorry?

MACRAMÉ: The past is tedious enough without adding the tedium of the future. On Sumitim Twelve G there are prophets who know the future inside and out, and they sit around on cushions and groan from boredom.

Driven by curiosity, I got down on all fours when Siphon and the macramé moved on, and put my ear to the crack in the tile next to the radiator. "Do you really play chess?" I whispered. I pictured the tiny chess master in the crack as a hermit in his cave, stroking a long, white beard.

The reply, unfortunately, was so extremely faint that I could not make it out, even with the volume of the peripheral turned up full (which I did mentally).

I continued making the rounds of the macramés. Although no longer directly involved in what was taking place, I felt responsible and wanted to keep tabs on the progress of the invasion. Regardless of what the fleas or lice pointed out, the aliens had seen better—or worse—on Zipper Three or Moofnakorb, etc.

At the Komsomolyetz, when I returned, footsore, there was a disturbance at the desk. A lady wept and blew her nose. Her husband, it seems, without warning, giving no indication that anything was troubling him, had locked himself in the bathroom and with a razor blade opened both wrists in the tub. (Unpleasant thought. With the water never hot enough, the bleeding would take longer and hurt more.)

Although it was dark and snowing again, I decided to drop in on Tolya. I needed cheering up. But Tolya was in a bad mood, angry about something Yevdoxia Fyodorovna had said or done, and because Irena Matvyeyevna had taken Yevdoxia's side in the disagreement and not his. He was even angry with me. I attempted to get a conversation going, but he answered only in sullen monosyllables.

"You're not good company," I said.

He gave me a black look. "You're a traveler. You don't have to stay here—I do." Then he ran his fingers through his hair, rubbed his temples, and apologized with a weak smile. "Excuse me, Volley. I have a migraine."

That night, in bed, I was surrounded by more hallucinations than usual, and they were all awful. The medicine kept my pulse even, but the images put me on edge. I fell into an uneasy sleep and dreamt that I was on Grokhovoy Street. But this was not the Grokhovoy Street of Omsk; the trees were different, they had green fruit. I asked Irena Matvyeyevna for directions, but she was talking to Psylla (who wore a shawl). Heads bent in a secretive whisper, they did not want to be interrupted.

In the dream I said, to no one in particular, "I should at least know where I am." I tried to be patient. "Perhaps this will give you a clue," said a friendly letter carrier, pointing. I looked up and beheld, towering high above the sawmill, the shoemaker of Girre. He was (as I expected) thin as a string bean, and he crunched loudly on a carrot. "People are trying to sleep," I told him. He nodded, pocketed what was left of the carrot, and put in his mouth, instead, a stick of imported chewing gum.

"So this must be Chamzifa'ulbzi," I said to the letter carrier. But the letter carrier had turned into a bahezan. Flicking its tapered tail, the animal disappeared into the underbrush. I started home, not amused by the joke. Then an overweight gentleman in a fez emerged from behind the corner of a building and beckoned emphatically. "You must come to The Gastronome. The meeting begins in five minutes."

"What meeting?"

"The Prophets of Sumitim Twelve G are deciding the fate of the world."

It was still dark when I woke. Immediately I sensed that something had changed. I asked my conscience. It said, subdued, that the macramés were leaving.

"They can't do that!" I cried. "They haven't even begun to see our planet. All they've seen, for God's sake, is downtown Omsk." It was not fair.

I was to blame, of course. Stupid of me, stupid, to enlist the fleas. How could a flea—how could a *louse*—be expected to present the achievements of civilization? They were nearsighted, pedestrian vermin.

I hurried out, hoping that I might be able to change the minds of the macramés. But most of them—all except one—were gone. I saw the telltale ripples on the Om, which they used (however they did it) as their dimension portal.

"I had hoped you would stay longer," I said to the last macramé, a sad, pendulous clump of nondescript gray. My disappointment made it difficult for me to swallow. "We didn't have much to show you, I'm afraid."

The macramé answered in a hollow whistle. "We never stay long, anywhere. There is never that much to see."

"Why do you travel, then—if there is nothing new under this sun or any other?"

The macramé made a movement similar to a shrug. It began drifting down the embankment toward the steel-blue water. "Why, indeed," it muttered.

I stood staring at the empty river for a while. All

sorts of bad memories came to me, from my asylum days. The time, for example, when they tied me in a straitjacket and I couldn't use my arms to shield myself from the black dogs that kept leaping at me, their fangs like shark teeth. I turned my back to the icy wind that blew out of the northeast. The temperature was falling.

Facing south, down the main boulevard of Omsk, I noticed large things suspended in the few trees that grew at the center of the traffic circle a block away. At first I thought, with a flutter of hope, that they might be macramés remaining. But then, coming closer, I saw that they were people. It was the heavy coats that gave them so much bulk. They swayed, rotating slowly, in the wind.

An elderly man at the base of one of the trees was having difficulty. He could not toss his rope up high enough; it kept dropping from the limb he wanted. Catching sight of me on the sidewalk, he appealed; he waved his arm for me to approach. I sighed, crossed the street, and helped him with the rope.

"Thank you," he said, grabbing the end of it. "You're very kind."

I nodded and continued on my way, leaving him to do the knot as best he could. The intense cold made one's fingers numb, so he would be fumbling with it a while, impatient though he was to join the others on the tree. I felt sorry for him, with his white hair and wrinkles, but it didn't seem moral for me to help him with the knot, too.

Tolya was in, and more morose than ever. To brighten him up, I raised the subject of the Great Bondaryov. He sneered. "Bondaryov," he said, "is a careerist. He doesn't care a fig about the dance. All he cares about is his sports car."

"But you idolized him."

"It's the Siberian winters, Volley'nka. You have to idolize something. It's that or alcohol. I have dropped the ballet and taken up alcohol."

It was only then that I saw that he was drunk. He put a bottle of vodka between us, on the table, with a clunk. Three-quarters empty.

"Won't Irena Matvyeyevna mind? And Dorotyeya Vassilyevna?"

"Fuck Irena Matvyeyevna. And fuck Dorotyeya Vassilyevna."

(Fortunately they weren't around.)

"The only trouble is," Tolya went on, "the stuff hurts the stomach." He poured vodka into two cloudy juice glasses, spilling some. We clinked and drank. He was right: it was the worst possible rotgut. It smelled of spoiled fish.

"Russians are supposed to be famous for their vodka," I said, blinking, holding my stomach. There was a knife inside me.

"Oh, they make the best in the world, but the good vodka, Volley'shka, is all shipped out to the capitalists, for Western currency, or kept in the big-city hotels, for the tourists—for Western currency. Who comes to Omsk? Does Omsk have Western currency? Sorry. Excuse me. Bondaryov does not set his precious foot here."

He got up with a grunt, went over to his bed, and pulled out the trunk from under it. The autographed glossy of the Great Bondaryov was soon produced. Tolya asked me if I had a match.

"Don't burn it," I said. "You'll regret it later."

But he found a match and without a word set a corner of the picture on fire. He let it fall. It quickly shriveled on the table, giving off white smoke.

I was trying to think of something consoling to say when a shot rang out. A woman screamed; there was the noise of people running. A murder? Tolya wasn't interested; he refilled his glass and drank, throwing back his head. He winced, shuddered, and held his stomach. He took no notice of me as I left.

In the stairwell a group was talking. I recognized the athletic woman, Yevdoxia Fyodorovna, and the young Communist with acne. "I can't blame him," she was saying to another woman, whose hair was kerchiefed and who held a copper-colored carpet sweeper. "What did he have to live for?"

"Still, it made a mess," said the woman with the sweeper.

"What does *he* care?" said another woman. "He doesn't have to clean it up, she does."

"Brains, everywhere brains," said a teenager, as if it were a joke. But no one laughed.

Outside, it was snowing. I took a walk along a long row of factories. There was very little activity, not much traffic. No clanking or grinding, no smoke from the stacks. Was today a holiday of some sort? The large, square buildings stood like tombstones in the snow. The light was so dim, it felt more like dusk than the middle of the afternoon.

I had no goal. I didn't know what to do with myself.

Since the invasion was over now, I supposed that I should go home. Having failed miserably. (My conscience wouldn't speak; I could feel its resentment.) At least no harm had been done; the world would go on as before. The macramés were no doubt wending their way to their next stop, where they would be disappointed again in their eternal search for novelty.

What kept them going?

I returned to the Komsomolyetz, packed, paid my bill. The manager was not there; a younger man, distracted, took his place. I had to ask him three times to call a cab.

The cabdriver also was distracted. His name was Boris. He drummed his fingers on the steering wheel. "Boris," I asked, "what are we waiting for?" He didn't seem to hear me. "Boris?"

"Oh, yes," he said finally, with effort. "I was thinking."

"The airport," I reminded him.

"You want to go to the airport?" As if that were a new idea, hard to grasp.

"Surely you've taken people to the airport before."

He nodded slowly, started up the car, and pulled out into the street. But after a couple of blocks we came to a stop. There was a group of people milling in front of us and they didn't move out of the way.

"It must be an accident," I said.

"Another person jumped off the roof," said Boris. "They've been doing that a lot lately. It reminds me of a poem by Yesenin."

"Another suicide. . . ." (My fault?)

"The poem goes, Good-bye, my friend, good-bye . . ."

Suddenly I thought of Tolya. "Look," I said to the cabdriver, "let's make a quick detour. There's a person I want to check on before I leave. He's been depressed."

We turned around and went east, to Tolya's apartment building.

"And I am glad I breathed and trod the grass," Boris recited in a monotone as the entrance banner came into view:

50 YEARS OF THE UNION OF METALLURGY PRODUCTION
"CAUCASUS"

"Wait for me," I said, and jumped out and ran up the stairs. Why was I running? Departure time wasn't for three hours yet. (Better to sit at the airport, I had decided, than spend another minute in that miserable hotel.)

A strong smell of gas came from the landing on the fourth floor. Were people all putting their heads in ovens? Ha-ha. Out of breath, heart pounding, I continued up.

The door to Tolya's apartment was locked. I knocked, and knocked again. "Anybody home?" I asked through the door, surprised at the harshness of my voice. "Home" echoed up and down the hall. Oddly, no one came out to look. (Occupants of Soviet apartment houses are notoriously nosy.)

No one was in, and I should have left—the cab was waiting—but an irrational fear came over me and before I knew what I was doing, I was battering the door with my shoulder and, when my shoulder hurt too much, kicking with my full foot (so as not to break the toes). The door splintered a little, but held. Then, with one of the kicks, something snapped and the door swung open.

It was extremely cold in the apartment. No wonder: the windows were all wide open. I went to close them and saw, on the ground below, several bodies, like broken dolls. Were the remains of Irena Matvyeyevna down there among them? And Dorotyeya Vassilyevna? It didn't seem likely. Motherly types did not succumb easily to boredom.

Indeed, I turned and saw Irena Matvyeyevna, alive, sitting in a chair in the corner. Her hands were folded in her lap. She stared straight ahead with a drawn look that told me that what I had hoped would not happen had happened. I found Tolya in his room, on his bed, in an ungraceful, cramped position. There was ice on his face and beard, and his eyes were not closed all the way. The empty pill bottle on the floor had no label.

When I returned to the cab, the engine was still running but the driver was gone. The Yesenin poem probably did Boris in. Could I drive myself? I had never driven a car. (Not possible to get a license, for one with my condition.)

The car was a stick shift. It stalled a few times and bucked a lot before I managed to get it going. I went up on the sidewalk and scraped past a street sign, then hit the corner of a parked car, which broke some glass. A headlight. Gradually I caught on. Driving was not so difficult. Of course, the complete absence of traffic helped. I had the road to myself. Shifting wasn't necessary, as long as I stayed at a moderate speed.

The smoking Minotaur that appeared on the seat beside me made me jump a little, but I didn't lose control. "Nice try," I said, "but I was expecting something like that."

"Oh, well," said the Minotaur, and dissolved, unchagrined, as if it was only doing its job.

In Kazan there was a stopover, for some reason, of ten hours. A guide, seeing that I was an American, offered to show me the sights of the town. I told him that I really wasn't interested. Kazan, he explained to me, was an ancient Russian city. Some of the structures actually went back as far as the Tartar Yoke. Thirteenth-century architecture. He chided me. "You would rather sit here on a bench, in this drafty, unheated waiting room, and stare at the cinder block?"

"It makes no difference," I said.

He looked at me. "You are ill?"

I smiled and said nothing. He would be ill, too, when the influence of the macramés reached him, spreading slowly, in a widening circle, from Omsk.

The guide dragged me with him, swearing that he would not charge me a red cent even though all Americans were rich and owned two cars; he would prove to me that his unique Kazan was worth the trouble of seeing. I had to remind him more than once not to put his arm around me, because my shoulder, badly bruised, was painful.

The only thing about the town that struck me was the fact that it, too, had an oil refinery.

In a restaurant that the guide praised extravagantly and at length, we ate a heavy, overgarlicked meal, so that I was queasy even before I got on the plane. The flight to Moscow made me more airsick than I had ever been; I clenched my teeth the whole way.

A week later, a few days before Christmas, the death toll in the Soviet Union was on the news on television. According to TASS, it was an unprecedented epidemic caused by a mutated flu virus now under control. The American commentators speculated that it was really because of an accident in a biological warfare plant. More than fifty thousand people had died. It was probably more like a hundred and fifty thousand.

The human race would have perished completely, I later learned, if the fleas hadn't stepped in. The story was given to me by an emissary from the Allied Armies of Russian Parasites, a bedbug who called himself Corporal Cimick. Generals Siphon and Pulex, discerning the threat, had quickly mobilized their forces. (So they had decided that they needed us, after all. A world without people would certainly have been a cold, unfriendly place for them.) The fleas—and lice, and whatever else—had attacked the inhabitants of the areas around Omsk in untold numbers and with untold fury. They had swarmed with the awesome might of a biblical plague. The humans, reported Corporal Cimick, were made so miserable that they totally forgot the tedium of existence.

"And it helped, I suppose," I said, "that there was no flea soap to be had, or fumigating herbs, in the town."

"According to General Pulex," said Corporal Cimick, "a man requires a certain minimum in creature comforts and leisure time to be able to contemplate the taking of his own life."

"My compliments," I told the bedbug, "to Generals Siphon and Pulex. They had you travel all this way to convey your message?"

"It took only two weeks, sir, transferring from host to host."

"Well. I don't mean to be inhospitable, but . . ."

Corporal Cimick understood. He said he did not object to spending the night at a nearby motel before heading back to the Asian continent. He gave a little salute, which I could barely see, and was gone.

Akron

Against Klabtak and the Klabs, I didn't even need to use my peripheral for recruiting. I went straight to the authorities of the city and told them that I was a specialist in extraterrestrial invasion. Naturally they were skeptical. But the shock of the appearance of the Öht had loosened their grip enough on the everyday for them to listen, when I gave an account of my activities in Barrancabermeja and Omsk, instead of showing me the door. One of the mayor's assistants, Mr. Bostwick, even let me sit in his office while he did some checking on the phone.

He turned to me. His face was careworn. "You say that these damned file cabinets are *tourists*?"

"File cabinets?"

"That's what they look like. You mean you haven't seen them? They're all over the place."

From the bus station I had taken a cab to City Hall, paying little attention to my surroundings along the way. My mind was occupied by my recent problem with Bea. Things were progressing, in our relationship, to the point where one had to decide whether or not—

Mr. Bostwick went to the window, pointed. "There's one."

I looked over his shoulder. On the corner stood an alien. It was metallic, definitely file-cabinetish in appearance, though a little narrower toward the top. It appeared to be somewhat flexible.

"I guess I'd better go down and talk to it," I said.

"I thought you were going to get rid of them."

"To get rid of them," I explained, "I have to find out why they're here."

"Just be careful. They might be armed." Mr. Bostwick's nerves were making his right cheek twitch.

Klabtak was the name of the Öht on the corner, and he was full of praise for our planet. "The sky is such a lovely blue here," he said.

A lovely blue? Actually, above us there was a haze typical of all cities and industrial centers. The sky over Akron was more white-gray than blue.

"The colors on your world must be pale," I hazarded.

"I wouldn't say pale," said Klabtak, "but different, yes. Every world is unique."

I asked him about his race and what brought them to Ohio. Klabtak didn't mind answering. He was an agreeable, pleasant being. But, like a child, he had difficulty keeping down his excitement at having arrived at his destination; as he talked, he was constantly distracted by some new wonder that came to his attention. (And just about everything, it seemed, even a stray dog that limped, was a new wonder.)

The Klabs were a form of machine life from another galaxy in our cluster (so we were practically neighbors), and their purpose in traveling was to see—and record—as much of the Creator's Creation as possible before it was ruined by the Eventual Niff and Harg. When I asked what the Eventual Niff and Harg was, Klabtak waved a small accordion appendage and said cheerfully that it was such a long way off, it wasn't worth worrying about.

But how would this Eventual Niff and Harg ruin the Creator's Creation, I wanted to know. Was this a synonym for destruction? For entropy? (I had recently read about entropy in a book from the library.) Klabtak, restless, said vaguely that there was a race, a superrace, that someday, coming from a great distance and between dimensions, would convert our entire continuum to its pattern, a pattern in which nothing would be unique anymore or have value.

(The Klabs' recording, by the way, took place automatically and simultaneously with their seeing. Each Klab accumulated his impressions, every detail, in internal spools that could be taken out and stored—and viewed by others—at a central location. In a sense, then, they *were* file cabinets. File cabinets with cameras.)

Klabtak excused himself. Much as he enjoyed talking to me, there was something he *couldn't* miss: on the other side of the street a man on a scaffold was touching up the paint in an old-fashioned sign that occupied a brick wall. Beneath the letters

HYMAN'S WHOLE WHEAT

were a large loaf of sliced bread, at an angle, and, a little to the right and below that, the curly heads of a girl and boy. The girl and boy were looking up at the bread and beaming in anticipation.

Was it the ad or the man painting that captivated Klabtak? Perhaps both. The alien went to a spot on the sidewalk by the scaffold and stood rooted, his odd metallic body bent back and his face (a collection of buttons and knobs) upturned.

The picture itself, of the bread and the children, was really quite poor. Unprofessional. That it should be the object of adoration was comical. (And the work-man-painter was no bargain, either: his pants were baggy, his clothes and shoes were of course spattered, and he needed a shave.) Then I noticed a few other Klabs, in different places up and down the street, in similar postures of raptness before similarly inappropriate shrines.

"Well?" said Mr. Bostwick when I returned.

"They're here for beauty," I told him.

"Beauty?"

Beauty wasn't the right word. "They're here for experience. They want to experience many things. Everything."

"What's there to experience in Akron?" Mr. Bostwick wondered aloud.

"They can make an experience out of a drainpipe," I said. "Whatever they see—it doesn't matter what it is—they think it's wonderful." Which sounded embarrassingly like something from one of those Hare Krishna fliers, but it was the best I could do.

Mr. Bostwick sighed, took off his glasses, slowly rubbed the inside corners of his eyes. "So they're a nuisance rather than a menace."

"They could be a menace, too, in some way unforeseen. That seems to happen with these invasions."

"Menace or nuisance, how do we get rid of them? What do I tell the mayor? You're supposed to be the expert, yes?"

Actually, I did have an idea, from the painted sign presenting Hyman's Whole Wheat. Commercialism. The Klabs might be put off by people breathing down their necks to sell souvenirs. "Let out the word," I said, "that these Öht are fantastically wealthy. They're dripping with wealth. Their planet is made of solid gold."

Mr. Bostwick sat up and put his glasses on again. "It is?"

"And their government says that whatever they don't spend here they have to pay seventy percent taxes on when they get back."

The stratagem was effective—and on a much larger scale, and with greater speed, than I expected. An army of vendors, salesmen, and television people sprang out of nowhere, overnight. There were almost as many of them as there were Klabs, and the traffic in Akron, a problem to begin with, became impossible. The mayor believed that the reason for this response was the economic slump that the nation was presently undergoing.

I was given an office. At first, the possession of an office tickled me. Sitting at my desk, I used my sleek console phone to call Lucille. She was not that interested in the latest invasion; she took me to task for not having gone out and bought myself new clothes, as I had promised. "Aside from the fact that you look like somebody on the dole or just out of an institution, Wally," she said, using her sharp voice, "it's bad for the self-image, and your self-image is what you need to work on. How can a person start a new life if he's not well-groomed and decently dressed?"

She had said the same thing before, last week, when she noticed the hole in the elbow of my sweater.

She would have taken me shopping herself, she told me, but was too busy. April was a tough month for the mentally disabled; a lot of hands needed to be held.

"I'll start looking for things while I'm here in Akron," I promised. "You'll be proud of me."

Ray, from down the hall, dropped by, complimented me on my appointment, and asked if I had any aspirin. He was all out. He popped aspirin like candy, because of his tension headaches. "We're taking a vacation this summer, no matter what, Nan and I," he said. "Minnesota, up in the lakes."

We talked, told jokes; then he had to get back to work. I sat alone at my desk and realized, after staring at the watercolor on the wall for five or ten minutes (an Oriental vase with violets), that I had nothing at all to do. I decided to take a walk.

Out of habit I headed for the river, which in this city was the Little Cuyahoga. No oil refineries were in sight. A Klab stood transfixed at the entrance to an alley, contemplating something. The object of his attention turned out to be nothing other than a pair of slanted cellar doors, wood, very worn and grimy, joined by a rusted hasp. The hasp was secured with a stick instead of a padlock.

"What interests you about this?" I asked the Klab.

The Klab sighed and shook his head slowly: his heart—or whatever served the file-cabinet being for a heart—was too full for words. I left him, embarrassed at having intruded, and continued down the avenue.

There were Klabs everywhere, and all were riveted on something and grooving with the same beatitude.

"I wish," murmured one Klab to himself, looking up at a traffic light, "that the moment could last forever."

"You like how the colors change?" I asked.

"No," he replied. "That *is* nice, but I mean the way the cables rock—so faintly, with such subtle rhythm—in the wind. I cannot express it."

"And the cables will not do that," I asked, "after the Eventual Niff and Harg?"

He regarded me through a retractable, segmented-sinuous periscope that I had not noticed before. (Apparently the Klabs had parts that could be attached and detached at will—or else that emerged and disappeared via little trapdoors.) "Of course the cables will rock in the wind then. But, you see, there will be no one to appreciate it."

"All dead?"

"Not dead," he said. "You do not understand. But isn't it a pity, human—don't you agree?—to waste this all-precious present discussing such dusty abstract matters of the distant future?"

The End of the World didn't seem that dusty or abstract to me, but it was probably impolite to pursue the subject. The creature, obviously, wanted to think positively. I walked on, letting him commune in peace with his traffic-light cable.

At the river I turned north, along an expressway choked with cars. They were bumper-to-bumper in both directions. Some people were half out of their windows, snapping pictures of the aliens. Occasionally a Klab would face a picture-taker and for a moment the acquiring of impressions would be reciprocal.

A high, modern office building gleamed in the sun; a large Goodyear blimp floated over the city; a

billboard advertised an aristocratic gin. It was strange,
I thought, the way the scene changed so completely
every few blocks. As if there was not one Akron but
a hundred. Everything depended on the standpoint
of the observer. If I were to get down on my hands
and knees, I supposed, I would think the world con-
sisted of ants, gobs of spit, and pebbles. (And what
was Siphon doing now?)

As rapidly as it had shifted from old to new, Akron went from city to small town. I crossed a bridge
and entered an area of boutiques. A Klab, looking in
a display window at an unclothed, pink mannequin,
was accosted by a vendor. The vendor held a number
of items on a tray that was suspended from his shoulders with straps. He had a loud voice.

The man's beginning ploy was to introduce himself: Richard. He put out a meaty hand, but was at a
loss what to shake. The Klab, distracted from his con-
templation of the dummy, supplied an appendage
(for invaders, they were awfully obliging) and replied,
"Klabbik."

RICHARD: Welcome to Earth, Mr. Klabbik.

KLABBIK: Thank you.

RICHARD: Something to show the children on
your return? A present for the missus? I have replicas
of the Liberty Bell, genuine brass.

KLABBIK: An interesting misunderstanding. We
are not gendered.

RICHARD: I have postcards, friendship rings, these
little cats—cute, aren't they?

KLABBIK: Your hair, Richard, is a beautiful hue.

RICHARD: What? (With a laugh.) Oh, I'm a red-
head. They used to kid me at school.

KLABBIK: It's chestnut. And so fine, almost silky
—in strange contrast with the coarseness of the skin
and the hard features, Richard, of your face.

The vendor flashed a smile, muttered something
under his breath, and with a couple of quick nods
took his leave, to try his luck elsewhere.

It occurred to me suddenly that I had forgotten
to activate the peripheral to do the translating. Which
meant the Klabs were speaking English on their own.
I was impressed—but then remembered that they
were machines, after all. Going from language to language, for them, might be only a matter of changing
spools or disks, or cassettes, or whatever it was they
used to store vocabulary.

Another Klab, a block farther, was buttonholed
(figuratively speaking) by a news correspondent with
a microphone and a camera crew working out of a
van. The questions were of a financial nature. The
Klab had so much difficulty paying attention, he appeared obtuse. "This one's a dud," the reporter called
to his men, and they all got back into their van, losing
no time, and merged with the traffic.

What was the Klab intent on? I asked him. But
he turned to me with such reluctance that I did not
press the point. A bus chugged past with its destination on its forehead: CUYAHOGA FALLS. The fumes
were dreadful; bitter, like burnt garbage.

The appearance of a large department store
across the street reminded me of my need to buy a
wardrobe. Why put it off, I told myself. What else did
I have to do? And Lucille would be pleased. Also, it
would give me a chance to try out the new credit card.

I looked for shirts first. In the men's section there
was an aisle of nothing but shirts. But a number of

unexpected choices stopped me. What was the difference, for example, between the thirty-dollar shirts and the fifteen-dollar shirts, besides the brand name and the price? Which material was better? What colors, what patterns were more appropriate for me? What style? And what was my size? I tried to find a salesman to help me out, but there were none in sight, only a crabbed lady ringing up purchases—and to talk to her, I would have to wait on a very long line. The store was crowded. There was a Klab, preoccupied, looking sadly out of place, at the cologne counter.

It would make more sense, I decided, for me to go to a men's clothing store, where they would charge more but I could get advice. I located one nearby, on the corner. The salesman who waited on me, however, gave me an uneasy feeling. His hair was sleeked down on his skull and he had a mustache so extremely thin, it was little more than a pencil line. His eyes were jaded, his skin pasty. How could such a person be trusted? Sure enough, he recommended the most expensive things in the store. And whatever I suggested he agreed with, approved of, in a tone as insincere as the smile on his face.

Dust motes caught in a ray of sunlight circled slowly. For a moment, watching them, I forgot where I was.

"Excuse me," I said.

"You mentioned socks?" prompted the salesman. "Slacks? A belt?"

"Do you think three shirts will be enough?"

"You might include a dress shirt." And a sports jacket. Or would I consider, instead, a suit? They had some nice three-piece suits. (Would Lucille like a three-piece suit, or would she laugh at me?)

The selecting, measuring, and trying on took forever. But the improvement in the mirror was astonishing.

The only items I knew anything about, from my inventory days at the McPhee department store, were handkerchiefs and underwear. As far as the handkerchiefs and underwear went, the prices *were* higher here, but not criminally. My confidence increased, and the money bothered me less and less. I did not even blink at the fact that the shoes—very comfortable—were more than fifty dollars. That was what the credit card was for. There would be no embarrassment. I left smoothly, my arms full of rustling bundles, and ate lunch at a Chinese restaurant.

I sipped the soup with care, not wanting to spatter my new shirt; I dabbed my lips with the linen napkin.

Then I found myself staring at the weave of the cloth and thinking dreamy things about texture and suppleness. Was this another case of mental infection from the Öht? My eyes strayed inappropriately. A detail would claim my attention for no reason. The mole on the waiter's neck. The interlocking pink-and-maroon flowers of the wallpaper. But possibly I was just tired from the shopping.

At the office I hardly had a chance to put my packages on the desk when Mr. Bostwick came in, both hands outstretched, to congratulate me. Klabtak and the Klabs, apparently, had left, and the credit was going to my idea of employing vendors. Mr. Bostwick clapped me on the back. There was some froth at the corners of his lips as he talked.

They insisted on having a public ceremony to present me with a key to the city. At the same time I was told that a lot of people were furious with me for having interfered, the file cabinets from Planet X being considered a source of inestimable wealth and consequently a once-in-a-lifetime opportunity. There was talk of lawsuits, even, but the mayor laughed and said not to worry. He invited me to stay at his house.

In the limousine the mayor explained to me the problems facing Akron. I nodded sympathetically, which made a good impression. When he asked me for my opinion, I shook my head and sighed, and that made an even better impression. The mayor patted me on the knee.

My room was enormous; the walls were a lovely pastel aquamarine, and there were interesting pen-and-ink sketches of English countryside scenes with spreading brambles and old fences.

We were served, at supper, by actual servants. The man servant was stiff and sour, exactly like a bank teller in the movies; the woman servant wore her hair in a bun, kept her jaw set, wore no makeup, and didn't seem to need to breathe.

The mayor's wife was old—at first I thought the lady was his mother. She smiled at me frequently, and I smiled back, but without knowing what the smiles meant (they were not particularly friendly).

There was no question but that Lucille was right about the clothes. I would have been painfully out of place in the mayor's dining room wearing my old shirt, pants, and shoes, whereas now I fit in, more or less. I was presentable. And I would look fine at the public ceremony tomorrow, with my three-piece suit and silk tie.

On the way to bed I stopped and opened a door, thinking it was a bathroom, but it was someone else's room. I saw a white, extremely smooth female thigh. I shut the door quickly, mumbling, "Excuse me." Was the woman part of the mayor's family, or a friend, or another servant? But what did it matter to me what she was? It had been an honest mistake, a wrong door, no one was to blame.

The next day, we went back to City Hall in the limousine. In an antechamber I shook hands with about a dozen men, one of whom (because of the goatee) reminded me of Dr. Gross, and then we had to file into a large, echoing room where there were stagehands and television cameras. The mayor made a speech. At a prearranged signal, I approached to receive the key to Akron.

It was difficult to concentrate, perhaps because I was nervous. I thought about the thigh. About how, when Bea and I were watching television at her apartment, during one of the shampoo commercials, we began kissing. Marriage between us, two mental defectives, was of course out of the question. Lucille, on the other hand . . .

Receiving the key and trying to hold it in a way that was not suggestive, I said a few words of thanks into the microphone. Then I added a caution, though I don't think anyone was paying attention, about the possibility of aftereffects from the invasion. The mayor shook my hand again, and a big luncheon followed. Plates of smoked fish, white and pink, and bowls of olives, celery, and radishes were arranged up and down the long table. I had never seen a tablecloth so soft and snowy. The water goblets glittered, throwing off little rainbows.

The first sign of trouble was from Ray. In the hall, the next day, he came over and put his hand on my shoulder. I noticed that he was unshaven, and his shirt was wrinkled. His eyes, also, didn't focus right.

"You're sick?" I asked.

He smiled. "No, no, just leaving." When I gave

him a puzzled look, he explained, "Getting away from it all."

"Ah, Minnesota, the vacation."

He smiled pityingly, or tenderly—it was a disconcertingly personal smile, as if somehow we had become intimate friends. "No," he said, with a lilt not typical of him. "One's own backyard is good enough, when the curtains of the world are drawn apart."

Then there was the man in the park with the briefcase. The man looked like an executive: a very dignified face, jowls, thick glasses. But, sitting on the bench, he wasn't resting the way executives rested— with a straight spine, head up, between conferences, occasionally checking the time. Taking his therapeutic fifteen minutes of air or nature like a dose of medicine.

Instead, he was bent over his briefcase, caressing and sniffing the leather. I looked away in embarrassment.

And in the elevator, one of the clerks sang in a soft voice and didn't get off at the top floor, and was still there, singing the same way, half an hour later, when I went down. I remarked to Mary, the receptionist in the lobby, that the clerk was using the elevator like his shower at home. Instead of laughing, she looked up at me, removed her glasses, and said, musing, that that was an interesting metaphor.

Over the phone Lucille sounded pleased when I told her that I had completed buying my wardrobe and had been well-dressed and groomed for my appearance on television.

Things wound down quickly after the excitement. The traffic thinned out. No one even talked about the wealthy file cabinets. Baseball was in the news, a big ship sank off the coast of California, and Turkey was having a crisis. I kept feeling that the day was Sunday, although it was only Tuesday. The banks were open and the mail trucks were moving, yet everyone on the street seemed relaxed and slightly blurred, as on the first really balmy day of spring.

"My head's untied," said a lady in a doughnut shop where I was having lunch. Many of us nodded, knowing exactly what she meant and appreciating the expression of it. It was the effect of the Klabs, no doubt, but surely in this case it was an effect that was beneficial. People would not commit suicide because of it, as with the macramés, or run amok and make mayhem, as with the green gourds. If anything, people would be finer, nobler, their eyes open to the beauty surrounding them.

Before leaving, I needed to buy a second suitcase to hold all my new clothes. The salesgirl in the luggage department was thin, had short, dark hair, and a smile so sweet that it was like sunlight. I could not take my eyes off her face.

"It doesn't have to be that durable," I said. "I'm only going on the bus."

She showed me several different suitcases at different prices, but I was too deeply in love with her to hear. I wanted to touch her arm. I wanted to press her to me and kiss her on the lips. She went on about the zippers and the waterproofing. I paid with my credit card, having no idea what I had bought, and told her silently, with a look that I put my whole heart into, that I would never forget her. She thanked me, handed me the suitcase and my receipt, and turned to the next customer.

There was a flood outside; a hydrant had broken, and no one was working on it. It was necessary to go ankle-deep in cold water to reach the other curb. I laughed, feeling like an irresponsible kid in bad weather. But would my new, over-fifty-dollar shoes be ruined? As soon as I got back to the office, I took them off, stuffed them with paper from the waste-basket, and put them near the register to dry (though I wasn't sure the heat was on).

I walked down the hall, socks squishing, leaving a trail of wet prints, to Mr. Bostwick's office, but nobody was in, not even Mrs. Hartley. Was today a state or local holiday? Only Mort's light was on. I went over to his cubicle. He was reading a book.

"Mort," I said. "Where's Mr. Bostwick?"

He shrugged.

"Where is everybody?" I asked him.

He lifted his eyes from the book and regarded me. "What is the problem, Wally?"

"I have to pick up my check from Mr. Bostwick."

Mort pursed his lips, as if considering the theory of relativity.

I left him. Even Mort, who didn't have an impractical bone in his body, was not all there, from the Klabs. It was as if everyone was underwater. You couldn't really communicate. I imagined two people at the bottom of an aquarium trying to hold a conversation. Gorgeous angelfish and iridescent tetras kept flicking in and out between them, in front of their faces, while their slow-motion voices gurgled away nine-tenths of the sense of every sentence.

And the hair on the top of their heads floated and snaked. Seaweed, in a chorus line, doing the hula. I found myself standing in a different room. What was I doing there? What was I thinking about? Seaweed?

With a suitcase in either hand, and my shoes still

soaked—no, the heat was not on today—I went down to one of the telephone booths in the lobby, to see if I could find Mr. Bostwick in the directory. I did find him—his first name was Henry, middle initial E—but no one answered. I rang eight times. I decided, having the feeling that things were at loose ends and getting looser, to drop in on the man at home, in person. Unannounced. Otherwise, good-bye check.

I took a cab. The driver reminded me of Boris, the driver in Omsk. This driver didn't recite poetry and wasn't glassy-eyed, but his head turned in every direction except straight ahead. We had several near-accidents, one by a souvenir shop whose window was filled with unblinking teddy bears. Finally, I asked him to let me out on a road where a row of old mansions faced a wooded lake. A sign said:

SAND RUN PARKWAY

The maple trees, I observed, were beginning to bud. Pale yellow-green. There were several birds' nests visible, not yet occupied, but they would be in another week or two. I walked.

It struck me that I had not paid the cabdriver. It must have slipped his mind, also.

Mr. Bostwick lived in a large house—red brick, white shutters, thick hedges, chimney—at the end of a rustic lane. His salary, I thought, must be considerable. The door knocker was brass, heavy in the hand, and made a deep, solid sound when it struck.

Mrs. Bostwick, all gray, invited me in. She never stopped smiling.

"Would you like something to eat?" she offered.

"No, thank you," I said. I put my suitcases down

in the vestibule, where there were hanging plants. "Is Mr. Bostwick in?"

"You've come to see Henry," she said, pleased, leading me to the kitchen. "How about some coffee and a Danish?"

"I'm not hungry, Mrs. Bostwick."

"It's good to get something in you." Smiling, she sat me down at a small, circular, wrought-iron table.

It was true that I hadn't had breakfast. Actually, I had missed lunch, too. There was so much going on. The Danish was surprisingly good. Mrs. Bostwick told me about the bakery she used to go to on the other side of Metropolitan Park—now, unfortunately, taken over by a chain.

"Their bread," she said, "was out of this world. The smell—divine."

The coffee, too, was good. But I needed to see Mr. Bostwick, I reminded her.

"The coffee," she said, "has chicory in it. Would you care for more, young man?" Then she sighed, seeing that I was determined. "You can *see* Mr. Bostwick, of course, but I don't think that you will be able to *talk* to him."

In the living room Mr. Bostwick, in only a bathrobe, was seated and sketching. The subject of his sketch—he threw frequent, intense looks at it, as if devouring it with his eyes—was the television set, which was not even turned on. I hardly recognized him. His glasses were crooked on his nose, and his hair went in every direction.

"Excuse me, Mr. Bostwick," I said. But it was obvious that he could not hear me. He was in a creative transport.

I asked Mrs. Bostwick, in a whisper, if her husband had ever shown an interest in art or drawing.

"Oh, no," she said. "Henry was always too busy for that sort of thing. Little did I dream, all those years—he must have bottled it up."

I noticed that his hand, holding the pencil, trembled. From emotion, or was he ill?

Mrs. Bostwick saw that I noticed the hand. "Yes," she explained, still smiling, "he is growing quite weak. He hasn't eaten in I don't know how long, poor dear."

I was going to suggest that, if this continued, she take him to a hospital, where they could force-feed him. Then I remembered Looie, whose cell was next to mine one year, and how they kept force-feeding him with a tube, and how he was always making himself vomit afterward.

But Mr. Bostwick's gray-haired wife seemed more proud than distressed. "Look at him," she said in a hushed voice. "Isn't he beautiful? You can see his soul in his face."

Jinn

This role of guardian was getting depressing. The waves of Öht had been repulsed, so far, more or less—that was true. Not that I could take credit for it in every case. In Omsk, the world was saved in spite of, not because of me. (My conscience was no longer on speaking terms with me over that one.)

But what kind of guardian was it, by any definition, who permitted people to perish in such great numbers? In the state of Ohio nearly a million, men, women, and children, starved to death. These were middle-class Americans, not foreigners, migrant farmers, or disadvantaged minorities. The president had to quarantine an enormous area—from Niagara Falls to Indianapolis, from Grand Rapids to Roanoke—to contain the disaster.

At least I was not held accountable—publicly, or by the authorities. In fact, the authorities appeared to have lost track of me, perhaps because things were in such a muddle at City Hall in Akron, which was (after all) ground zero. It must have been next to impossible to piece together the records of the invasion. And the media continued to be confused.

The thing that put the damper on the wildfire spread of aestheticism in our country was April 15, the income-tax deadline. The quarantine alone would never have worked: the soldiers stationed at the checkpoints were no less susceptible than executives, housewives, or salespeople. They became carriers themselves, their helmets and rifles providing no protection against the contagion.

Lucille insisted that I fill out my own return. Another first for me. "It's not complicated," she said. "All you do is follow the instructions." Reading the instructions, although supposedly they were simpler than they used to be, gave me a headache. In the lists of cases, I was not sure which case applied to me and which didn't. More than once I found that I was racking my brains over the wrong thing. The additions were tedious.

I was depressed, also, by the return of the hallucinations. There hadn't been a single one in Akron, which led me to hope that the problem was going away by itself somehow, contrary to what the medical experts said, and that I would be normal again, as I was at age ten. I even entertained thoughts of marriage to Bea. But when I went to take out the garbage, a blue jack-in-the-box head on a spring—Punchinello—popped up from the bag with a squeal and bit me on the nose. My heart almost stopped.

Lucille believed that I was out of sorts because of a reaction to my exposure to the different extraterrestrial cultures, one after another. To get my mind off the Öht, she made a date with me for the movies. "Wear jeans," she said.

The film was a science-fiction adventure with

swordplay. We had a milk shake afterward. Then, when she sat with me in her car, she looked straight at me suddenly and said that I should kiss her. Sheepishly, I gave her a peck on the cheek. "No," she said, annoyed, "like a man. Kiss like a man." We kissed fully then, embracing. I forgot that she was my doctor.

Now I would have to tell Bea that I couldn't be her boyfriend any longer. But Bea, before I could broach the subject, invited me to a party, and she was so excited, I hadn't the heart to refuse. This was her first party in years. A friend of hers from her childhood had recently rediscovered her—they met in a supermarket—and knew nothing about her problem.

There were five or six couples. The occasion was this Mary's engagement. The fiancé, Tim, a shy, tall individual with a protruding upper lip, was a geologist for an oil company. We drank champagne, played charades, laughed. All evening, Bea looked at me and smiled. She seemed happier even than Mary. How would I tell her?

I didn't. It was after twelve when we said good night to Mary and Tim. The person who drove us home made wrong turns and swerved a lot. I was relieved when I was let off, finally, at my house.

I went to have milk and cookies, to take away the taste of the champagne, and saw a note for me on the kitchen counter. In a careless scrawl it said:

QUEEN MAUD MOUNTAINS

A gorilla burst in and began throttling me, its eyes like embers. I ignored the beast, but took an additional pill with my milk. What was going to happen, I wondered, with Bea and Lucille?

The next morning, I chatted with Mr. Tribovich.

The subject was fertilizer. He maintained that there was no comparison between chemicals and the natural product. "Phosphorus, nitrogen, phooey," he said. "Fifteen years ago, I go to the farm with a bucket, I get horseshit, all I can carry. The plants shoot up, you wouldn't believe it. An eggplant, *this* big. Nowadays you pay an arm and a leg for a bag of little pellets and it don't even smell." But years before I moved in, the farm was replaced by a development and a shopping center. Mr. Tribovich shook his head. He had deep creases at the corners of his eyes.

At the library I checked the index of one of the large international atlases. The Queen Maud Mountains were located in Antarctica, not far from the South Pole.

It was one thing to bundle up for Omsk—*this* was ridiculous. How did they expect me to survive at hundreds of degrees below zero? And how was I supposed to get myself there? Commercial planes didn't go to the South Pole. I would have to hire a plane. Not only a plane but also, for the final miles, a sled with dogs. Unless I got a helicopter to drop me off. And by the time I reached my destination—assuming I could scrape up the fantastic amount of money that would be needed, assuming I could get all the necessary permits and passports, which was a lot of assuming—I would be much too late. A week late, a month late. There was no point even in trying.

Could the peripheral overcome all these difficulties? Not likely. It didn't seem to be a dramatic intervener. Devious, rather. Indirect.

On the other hand, I could not believe that the Conservationists had not given me sufficient power to travel to the South Pole if I needed to. Since the Öht could land anywhere. I stepped into the phone booth that was in the lobby of the library, put a coin in the slot, and dialed peripheral.

"How about it?" I said into the receiver.

The phone gave a ping, returned my coin, and said: "No problem. But the energy source *is* limited. Blink twice and close your eyes when you want to see how much you've expended."

I blinked twice and closed my eyes, and saw, on the inside of the lids, an indicator like a gas gauge in a car. It registered full, more or less.

Encouraged, I went home and got an old khaki backpack out of the closet. I didn't bother with heavy clothing or foul-weather gear: where I was going, if the peripheral couldn't protect me from the elements, nothing would help. I took a couple of changes of underwear, toiletries, and a paperback I had been reading—a science-fiction novel about a planet where all the inhabitants were under tremendous gravity. (The gravity was not natural, it was created by an evil race of overlords, but the hero was getting to the bottom of the conspiracy. At the end—I had peeked— there was saving-the-day and boy-gets-girl.)

The only item I bought for the trip was a pair of goggles from the army-navy surplus store around the corner, to protect my eyes from the wind. After supper, when it was dark, I put on the backpack, tightened the straps, and took off. I went quickly, vertically, from my bedroom window, which faced the back, to reduce the chance of being seen. One or two witnesses wouldn't matter—it would be assumed that they had been drinking. I had in mind those whose attention was best avoided.

It took me a while to orient myself. At several hundred feet up, I didn't recognize any of the streets. Finally I figured that the big glow in the sky must be from the city, which was roughly east; therefore south had to be to my right. I climbed above the clouds, where the moon was very bright, and accelerated.

But the cold grew too intense and the wind too violent, tearing at my clothes. A shield was what I needed. I fashioned a bubble, adding a steering wheel, a seat, and a few controls. Nothing large or elaborate. It was only common sense to economize. I didn't want to run out of gas at an altitude of ten or twenty thousand feet. And who knew what would have to be done—what energy would be required—once I arrived?

The buffeting of the wind still was too great. I began to get motion-sick. There would be less air resistance higher up, I thought. In the stratosphere I would be able to reach the South Pole in a couple of hours—and (the main point) keep the entire flight under cover of night. Higher up, I saw the curvature of the Earth. A few rays of the sun came over the edge on one side. That was west.

But with no other clue of direction—beneath me lay a featureless cloudscape—navigation was a problem. I supposed I could shoot out into space and then locate Antarctica from there; the polar regions, bright white, would be recognizable even to an amateur eye. A simpler solution was to have a south-pointer. I created one inside the bubble, on the dashboard: a pale pink arrow in a dial. The moment it reversed itself,

I would know that I had passed the southernmost point of the globe.

The next hour, monotony. No sense of motion. I turned on a small reading light and opened my paperback to where I had left off. The hero was in a force-field dungeon but the heroine had a plan to free him. Unfortunately, with each page the story became more and more predictable. The writer had started off strong but was now growing tired of the whole thing and wanted to get to the end with as little trouble as possible.

I looked at the stars for a while. I had never seen so many. I thought about time and the universe, and that it didn't matter to the stars whether humanity winked out within a year or held on for another few thousand. What did a few thousand years matter to a star?

Would we make it or wouldn't we, through these odd alien invasions? I began to feel we wouldn't be the lucky "one out of ten." Just as I had that thought, the speaker in the bubble crackled, as if clearing its throat.

"Ankara, in about two hours," it said.

I understood immediately. This was not an announcement of my position over the Earth, but a notice of the next Öht landing. There was no way I could make it. In two hours I wouldn't even be at my first destination—and a hundred peripherals couldn't arrange for me to be in two places at the same time. I gritted my teeth. Might as well go down swinging.

The south-arrow brightened, so I put on the brakes and began my descent. When I dropped through the thick clouds, it was raining heavily. Rain, not snow—so I couldn't be that close to Antarctica. I stopped at a town, parked the bubble on a flat roof, made a raincoat for myself, and unobtrusively slipped down through the air to a store where I could buy a newspaper.

The store that I found was not open (this was after midnight), but with the peripheral I had no difficulty unlocking the door. From behind the gum-ball machine Mrs. Collins spat fire at me, but she had to be a figment. The year I was released, she passed away.

The printing on the magazines in the magazine rack was not Spanish—I had thought that I was somewhere in Argentina—but, surprisingly, English. Everything was in English. A look at the framed permit over the cash register told me that I was in Melbourne. Wasn't Melbourne in the wrong hemisphere? If I had overshot the South Pole and come up on the other side, then it ought to have been day here, not night.

At any rate, I filched a pie out of a display case on the lunch counter, not knowing when or how I would eat again, and hurried back to the bubble.

It was a dreary dawn when I reached the Adélie Coast. Lots of glaciers and mist, but no penguins. (I was thinking of using penguins this time.) I headed inland, bearing left, observing in the distance a flat stretch of white that must have been the Ross Ice Shelf.

The pie—pecan—was gummy and tasteless, unfortunately, like the worst institutional food. After two bites I chucked the thing out. What would an explorer think, finding it?

The Queen Maud Mountains finally hove into view. I scanned them with peripheral-made binoculars but saw no sign of life. But, then, I was still quite high. The bubble was not easy to land; the strong wind hurled it around. Finally, when I was a few hundred feet up, I dissolved it and went down the rest of the way by myself.

The air, even with the whipping wind, was not too cold. I looked in every direction. The scene was the same: mountains, all white, and not a footprint anywhere. Where were the Öht? I didn't have all day to find them. Even now, other Öht were arriving in Ankara.

Sheets of snow-spray, driven by the wind, made visibility poor. It was hard to tell, also, what was firm ground—or, rather, ice—and what was only the surface of a drift. Now and then, as I walked, I would sink in up to my waist or neck. "Take me to the nearest penguin colony," I told my peripheral. "I need assistance."

I was annoyed. Why should I have to tell it anything? It knew what I needed. Unless—could it be running low already? To check, I blinked twice and closed my eyes. Not that bad. But perhaps the constant effort of keeping me from freezing to death slowed the peripheral's performance of other tasks.

The penguins, around a bend, paid no attention to me. When I asked them if they had seen anything unusual, they shrugged noncommittally and turned away. I buttonholed one, the largest, and insisted. His name was Sven. Sven had indeed heard about the invasions but had noticed nothing out of the ordinary on the Hobbs Coast.

"The Hobbs Coast?" I said. "But this is the Queen Maud Mountains."

"The Queen Maud Mountains," replied Sven, raising a tapered flipper, "are eight hundred and fifty miles in *that* direction."

The peripheral, I realized, had followed instructions literally, transporting me to the nearest penguin colony.

"No matter," I said to Sven. "You and your people will accompany me back there."

"We'd rather not," Sven said, and would have departed if I hadn't held him.

I tried to get through to the old penguin. "Don't you understand? The world hangs in the balance."

Sven stood immobile for a minute. For two minutes. Then he looked up at me and said, with a firmness I would not have expected in a penguin: "The world can take a running jump, as far as we're concerned."

"It'll be a day or two, tops," I promised, "and then you can return to your isolationism."

I whisked them all with me to the Öht site, and we appeared on a slope facing another slope. Through the mist of the constant snow-spray I made out large, unnatural shapes. "Wait here," I said to Sven, and walked across.

Closer, I saw creatures that had stone pillars for legs, the bodies of lions, and the heads of polyps, scarlet or violet-rimmed and slightly transparent, with thin, waving tentacles on top for hair.

"Yg-Mu-Yg," said the creature in front.

"My name is Walter Griffith," I said, stepping forward.

"Mu-Lef-Lof," intoned the creature. "Yk-Yk-Yk."

Was this new variety of Öht so extremely alien that the peripheral couldn't translate its language? I tried again. "I'm sure, gentlemen, that there can be nothing of interest for you here. You see for yourselves what sort of place it is." I stretched out my arm, indicating.

But, indicating, I looked and saw that the scene was really quite peaceful. There were no cars, no gas stations, no signs, and no noise, except for the wind and the soft, barely audible hiss of millions of tiny ice crystals driven along the slope.

Perhaps the Öht, not sensitive to the cold, had come to these forsaken mountains for a rest.

"Mu-Yt-Mu," said the rock-lion-polyp. "Beg-Tof-Dek."

"I could use a rest myself," I sighed. "All this running around."

The South Pole was, if you looked at it in a certain way, a world of pillows. Of endless sheets, big, fluffy blankets, thick comforters. Everywhere white and inviting.

"Yk-Yk-Feg," said the rock-lion-polyp, concluding its statement, and the others all seemed to agree.

If *our* modern life was full of tension, fear, ulcers, and distasteful work, and not enough time to do it, how much more difficult, then, *their* life had to be, who were far more modern than we, whole light-years ahead of us in technology and aggravation.

But the memory of the countless Ohio dead roused me from my sympathy. Nothing, nothing was harmless about these invasions, not even the desire to snuggle into a nice drift and take a nap. I set my jaw, marched back to Sven, and gave him my orders. I wanted an army of bureaucrats. The penguins would plague our visitors with forms, visas, and official questionnaires. One couldn't be comfortable in a bed, I reasoned, if the bed required a permit, and the permit required an application, and the application required notarization.

I told them to step on it, too, nervous about Ankara.

It was immediately evident that the penguins weren't going to cooperate. They were inattentive. Several kept dropping the clipboards I created for them. Some, with white goggle markings on their black faces, which gave them a wild-silly look, would completely forget their assignment and go belly-sliding.

"The Öht won't believe you," I called, "if you do that."

Sven would not be overseer. He told me that the ones with the white goggles were young, two-year-olds, and you couldn't do a thing with two-year-olds, and penguins away from water got restless.

No point beating my head against a wall. Time was of the essence. I whisked the lot of them back to the Hobbs Coast, where they belonged, and put the clipboards, rubber stamps, vouchers, and other office paraphernalia into the hands of animated snowmen.

"And what happens, Wally," said an old-maid voice inside my head, "when you run out of gas here in the middle of Antarctica? You'll be a block of ice in a second."

"Shut up," I said.

We started with a small group of rock-lion-polyps that had made its way almost to the top of the northeastern ridge.

"Excuse me," I said, "but do you have a validated pass to hike in the Queen Maud Mountain National Preserve?"

The tallest rock-lion-polyp stood flat-footed and gave me a blank look, almost like a human being, then exchanged a few furtive (it seemed to me) monosyllables with a smaller rock-lion-polyp that was its wife or child. I turned the case over to the couple of snowmen accompanying me and moved on. The snowmen looked convincing in their uniforms, and their impassiveness suited the role well. Cops giving tickets.

"Dek-Yk-Mef," protested one rock-lion-polyp ensconced on a glacier. "Mu-Yg-Yt. Feg-Feg-Dek. Lof-Tof-Beg."

The snowman didn't blink. "I'm sorry, sir," it said, "but the fee can be paid only at headquarters."

The alien's polyp head turned an ominous blue. It was angry. Apparently it felt that there was no point wasting any more words, because suddenly a beam of light shot out and destroyed the snowman. All that remained of my official was a gray cap floating in the air and a blackened scrap of paper.

A good thing I hadn't used the penguins!

There were more such outbursts of temper—these rock-lion-polyps had been through a lot and badly needed the rest they had come in search of—but the snowmen were replaced, complete with uniforms and clipboards, as quickly as they were obliterated.

I was beginning to get cold—very cold, in fact. All this creating and animating and whisking must have put quite a strain on the peripheral. A drain on its power. How much of a drain? I blinked twice and closed my eyes. Well, I thought grimly, there are

worse ways to go. Becoming a block of ice isn't painful, at least.

How often, in Rosedale, when the green centipedes were coming after me, or the grinning bears on wheels, had I wished I could be asleep in bed? Life, it seemed to me then, was like one of those revolving cages in which squirrels ran their hearts out struggling to escape. The monsters would always be at my heels, and I would always be howling with my raw throat and throbbing head, and the whole thing would start over again the minute I opened my eyes in the morning.

Then Mrs. Sanders, I recalled, would help me out with the breathing exercises and by teaching me to repeat words to myself during the worst. It always made me feel better to hold her thin, white, cool hand.

"Mu-Mof-Yg," said a voice. It was a short rock-lion-polyp. The tone was reproachful.

"I know," I told it. "You're dead on your feet and just want to be left alone. But if we leave you alone, you see, before you know it our whole world will be sound asleep and there'll be no one to take out the garbage or go get the milk."

Not an unattractive prospect, actually. A sleeping world would have no propaganda, traffic jams, sirens, or income tax. Only rhythmic snoring from coast to coast.

The image was so comfortable that I dozed off

before I reached the next sentence. I dreamt that I was talking with a group of three children who were playing rock-paper-scissors, which reminded me of something, but I couldn't think of exactly what. "Who's winning?" I asked in a friendly way. One of the children looked up at me, a boy with a solemn face.

"Nobody wins at rock-paper-scissors," he explained, as if I were the child and not he. "Each time, you start over. It's like odds and evens."

I was embarrassed. "I didn't get a chance to play games much when I was growing up."

It didn't seem fair to me—it seemed positively cruel—that one could win ten times in a row, only to lose on the eleventh turn. The ten wins meant nothing, nothing at all—it was as if those ten wins had never been—when the rock crushed your scissors, the paper covered your rock, or the scissors cut your paper.

An owl, watching us from its limb, wearing goggles, said: "Sorry to interrupt, Wally, but the South Pole Öht have left and your peripheral, right now, is carrying you toward Turkey."

"Does it have enough fuel to make it?" I asked.

The children stared. They must have thought I was crazy.

"No," said the owl.

Just as I awoke, reluctantly, the peripheral began sputtering. We were over green fields and woods. It had been trying to reach the ground before giving out. The wind whistled in my ears—the protecting bubble was gone. I shut my eyes tight and clenched my teeth, awaiting the horrible plunge. Then something strong yanked at my shoulders. Over my head was a beautiful, rippling, white dome. The noble peripheral, before winking out completely, had changed my backpack into a parachute.

I landed safely, in a tree near an abandoned farm. The people whom I approached on a dirt road, after an hour's walk, spoke a little English—but I couldn't understand a word of their tongue. This brought home to me the fact that from now on I was entirely on my own.

A man with deep wrinkles across his forehead and salt-and-pepper hair smiled at me when I asked if this was Turkey (unfortunately, I didn't know the Turkish name for Turkey). No, he said, it was Umtali. Umtali. He pointed gracefully at a ridge of green mountains in the distance. That, Mozambique. Mozambique.

I wasn't even close.

An F

―――――

But even with the peripheral—and even with an endless supply of energy and no need to maintain a low profile—I wouldn't have had a chance, a prayer, against the Caraputanians.

These Öht came for education. They came with notebooks and pencils, like students, leaning forward, not wanting to miss a word. They were human in appearance, so human, in fact, that you had to look at one closely—and in the light—to tell that it was a Caraputanian. (The eyelashes did not curl out but interlocked, instead, when the lids were closed; and the Adam's apple was horizontal.)

In their eagerness to learn, the Caraputanians spread out almost immediately over the entire globe. There were even a few of them in Harare when I arrived, a week later, in the police van. (The police were convinced that I was a spy or one of those soldier-of-fortune mercenaries, considering the parachute and my total lack of personal identification. I had neglected to take my wallet when I departed for the South Pole. How could I have known that I would need it? Embarking on fantastic excursions, one doesn't think to take along a driver's license, which I didn't have anyway.)

By coincidence, I shared a cell with an alien. He spoke English. He had thrown suspicion on himself by asking a great number of questions and, like me, by his lack of identification.

"Is imprisonment common here?" he asked me. "What percentage, do you think, of the population—"

I had no idea. One percent? One tenth of one percent?

He asked me the reasons for imprisonment.

"Wrongdoing, mainly," I answered. "We also put people away—confine them—if they're mentally ill." I began to think of all the other circumstances in which individuals were deprived of freedom—at least, of their freedom of movement. A child had to be in school; a patient had to be in the hospital; a soldier had to be wherever they put him.

We got into a long conversation on the subject. Talking, I hardly noticed the awful supper they gave us—dry, gristly meat with something like creamed corn—and it was only when it was time to go to sleep that I remembered that I had had a few questions of my own to put to the Caraputanian. Such as what brought him to Earth. And why learning about us was so important to him. (Was his reason anything like that of the Klabs?)

But another problem took my attention: my pulse was up. I had run out of pills, and the hallucinations, waiting for their chance, like Indians in ambush, came roaring out of the woodwork. The breathing exercises helped. I had to concentrate to avoid tightening up.

Particularly troublesome was a crow with the

face of a doll—rubbery pink—instead of a beak. It perched above my head all night and laughed. The laughter was not the usual maniacal monster noise, but intelligent, pointed: I had made or was making or was about to make a fool of myself once again.

The Caraputanian, in the morning, questioned me about bricks and mortar. He was regarding the wall of our cell.

"What difference does it make," I said, annoyed, because I had a headache from the night, "how the wall was made, if it keeps us in?"

Arrows kept thwacking into me during breakfast (lukewarm, greasy oatmeal); the Caraputanian, observant, asked me why I flinched. I explained to him my biochemical-neurological problem, using the language of Dr. Gross.

Chewing thoughtfully, he took notes in his notebook. I twisted my neck to see. I was about to ask him what he was writing, and why, but he asked me what the people on our planet did when they weren't satisfied with their minds.

I didn't understand the question.

One of the guards came in and took us to a room where we were interrogated. The interrogation, thank goodness, was without torture. I repeated my story and gave Lucille (name, address, phone number) as a reference, but not believing that they would go to the expense of calling her from Africa. The interrogator seemed to be a decent person: he wore a regular suit and tie, not a uniform, and had no nervous tic or typically sinister mustache.

"Mr. Griffith," he said, sympathetically, "you do not expect us to swallow your tale."

My tale: I had claimed that I was a photographer for an American magazine and was assigned to cover the national park systems in this part of the world. But I knew embarrassingly little, not only about the parks but about American magazines and even photography. Trying to supply specifics, I kept halting, correcting myself, scratching my head, saying that I couldn't remember or wasn't sure.

And to explain the parachute, I got myself out on such a farfetched limb, sweating, that a five-year-old could have done better. The interrogator said: "It appears to me that you are not here for any mischief, Mr. Griffith, but indeed you are a strange bird." He laughed. I laughed, too, relieved.

"What steps does your society take," inquired the Caraputanian, "to protect itself against individuals that do mischief?"

The interrogator turned to look at him.

The question was tactless, considering.

"There are fines," said the interrogator at last, coldly. "There is incarceration. And, if the mischief is grave enough to warrant it, there is execution."

"No surgical procedures?" asked the Caraputanian.

"In Harare," said the interrogator, smiling but (I thought) offended, "we do not castrate rapists, cut off the hands of thieves, or rip out the tongues of blasphemers."

The Caraputanian nodded and jotted down something in his notebook.

"May I see that?" said the interrogator, holding out his hand. The Caraputanian did not object. The interrogator leafed through the alien's booklet, lips pursed. "It is in code, I see."

"Actually," I said, "it's a foreign language. Very foreign."

"Do mischief-making individuals use code, as a rule?" the Caraputanian asked.

The interrogator looked at him sharply. "Do you mock me?"

The Caraputanian considered for a moment. "What purpose," he asked, "would be served by mocking you?"

"Many persons express their defiance of the authorities by mocking."

"Have the authorities given them cause to do this?"

The interrogator became dark in the face. He was tempted—it was obvious—to do or say something hostile. He struggled with himself and finally managed a smile that was civil.

"It is very amusing," he said, "that here you ask all the questions and not I."

"How else is one to learn?" replied the Caraputanian.

"Yes, but in that case how are we to learn about *you*?"

"I am not here for you to learn about me," the Caraputanian told him. "I am here to learn about you."

The interrogator cleared his throat, drummed his fingers on the desk, then turned to me and asked me what my plans were in Zimbabwe. I said that originally I was headed for Ankara but there was no point in that now. That all I wanted to do was get back to Wayne, New Jersey (and try to live out as much of my private life as possible before the world ended).

(I didn't see yet how these latest Öht would work our destruction, but I could tell that they would and that they were invincible. They were invincible because there was nothing to manipulate them with. Education-bent, they could not be bored, offended, or in any way discouraged. Whatever happened—good, bad, indifferent—was grist for their notebooks.)

"We will leave you to your own devices, Mr. Griffith," said the interrogator. "I suggest that you do return to your native country. As for you, sir—" he said, addressing the Caraputanian, "we will detain you."

"For what length of time?" asked the Caraputanian.

"That depends."

I took the Caraputanian aside and whispered to him: "Once you cooperate with him, I think he'll let you go. He's not the high-handed type."

"And what would he do," asked the Caraputanian, "if he were the high-handed type?"

"Oh, any number of things," I said, but suddenly didn't feel like unfolding more of our human weaknesses before the alien. Human beings were not bugs on a slide, to be studied.

It was with a flicker of pleasure, even, that I saw the Caraputanian escorted back to jail, the guard gripping his arm.

My only problem now, in getting home, was money. I was reluctant to borrow from Lucille. It was a lot to borrow. Leaving the police station, I took a walk.

A pallid individual on a street corner accosted me, but I kept walking. He followed, determined, for some reason, to strike up a conversation. His name was Frumzig (Frumzig?) and he was connected with a newspaper. What a shame, he said, that there was such a shortage of native speakers of English.

(Frumzig's own English was heavily accented.) I pointed out to this Frumzig that many and in fact most of the signs around us were in English, but he waved impatiently and said that he was not talking about the official English but the real King's-English article.

"I'm an American," I said, walking briskly, increasing my pace. "We don't have kings."

"Wonderful," he said. "You grew up speaking the language. Now, some of these new people here have the grammar A-1 perfect, but you can tell they didn't grow up speaking it." Frumzig made a grimace.

A train out of nowhere tried to run me down. The image was even accompanied with sound effects and the smell of smoke. I took deep breaths.

"One of them," Frumzig was saying, "works for us as a reporter. He sticks his nose into everything. You would think that that is good, for a reporter. But the man is overzealous. You would not believe it. The editor sends him out to cover the dedication of a church, we are talking about an inch or two of print, no more, and Ralph—his name is Ralph—comes back with more than a hundred pages, single-spaced, and even that, he complains, doesn't do justice." Frumzig patted the sweat off his pasty brow with a handkerchief.

"It sounds like a joke," he went on, still keeping up with me, "but I assure you that it is really a great pain in the ass, as you Americans say. We would fire him, but there is a dreadful shortage of good English speakers."

I stopped and turned to him. "You're not offering me a job, are you?"

Frumzig was indeed. He gave me such a look of delight that I was tempted, for a moment, to hit him in the face. I began walking again, and he trotted after, but his excited words were drowned out by another train whistle. I gritted my teeth and defied the phantom train head-on, but Frumzig with unexpected energy pulled me back by the arm from the tracks. A gust of hot, sour wind. This train was real, not imaginary.

A row of passengers, rumbling past, looked down at me from their windows.

To be polite, I thanked Frumzig for saving my life. I even went so far as to shake his hand. "My mind has been on a lot of things lately," I explained, resisting the impulse to wipe my hand afterward on my pants.

The pay wasn't great, but the living expenses were low. I was able to pocket most of what I brought home. In three months, I calculated, I would have enough to return to the States under my own steam. Frumzig put me up in a cubbyhole of a room at the back of his mother's house. She was a large-boned woman with an unnaturally wide mouth. Long black hairs hung from her upper lip and chin. She never spoke. When I said good morning to her at the breakfast table, she grunted and looked away.

But the house was close to the newspaper office, within walking distance, and my canvas cot—which occupied most of my room when I opened it—was comfortable enough. The only problem was the strong bleach smell that came periodically from the laundry next door. Because of the smell, I spent most of my free time at the Harare Public Library, where there was a pleasant solarium with mosaics and benches. They had plenty of books in English, the classics as well as light reading.

My main function, on the paper, was to supply

idioms. Mr. Mtimkulu loved idioms. He would nod vigorously and grin, reading the revised copy, and at least once a day, when he passed me, he would clap me on the arm and say, "Keep up the good work, Wally." Frumzig told me that Mr. Mtimkulu was in competition with another English-language paper in Harare run by an old archrival of Mr. Mtimkulu called Benjamin Nyikadzinashe. Having me on the staff was being one up on Nyikadzinashe.

If a reporter had written, "The number of color television sets in Zimbabwe increased this year to 4,500, from last year's figure of 2,200," I would change it to something like, "Color TVs in Zimbabwe better than doubled this year." "An unknown person broke into the house of Mr. Hifer Mzilikazi late last night, according to police authorities, and took several family heirlooms," might become, "Burglars struck Hifer Mzilikazi's place late last night and made off with, etc." It was easy work, and the reporters and editors were all friendly, with the exception of Ralph, who was too occupied to pass the time of day with anyone.

Ralph, as I had guessed from what Frumzig said, was a Caraputanian. He was constantly getting stories. And often, if someone else came in with a story, Ralph would perk up his ears, drop everything, and ask a million questions that no one knew the answers to; then he would dash out to get "more information." He was still working on a dozen stories that had been completed, printed a week ago or more, and completely forgotten. Mr. Mtimkulu sometimes gave him, reluctantly, an update column. The news editor, George Ndlovu, groaned when Ralph plunked down the pages and pages of copy on his desk.

Curious, I took a look one day at one of Ralph's

stories. About the new minister of the interior's dog-breeding hobby, it contained an awesome number of facts. The detail was such that if one were a god (this was the thought that occurred to me), one could almost rely on Ralph's text to re-create the whole reality in question. Where did the Caraputanian get his information? I asked him.

"Every event," he told me seriously, "leaves a variety of traces. And where there are gaps in the record, one can use reasoning."

"You mean," I said, shocked, "that some of your facts are just guesswork?"

"Oh, no," he said. "Reasoning is not guessing, it is a hundred-percent scientific. Consider, for example, the star of your planetary system. How do you know its diameter and temperature? Only by reasoning."

"We have instruments," I said, "that measure it."

Ralph shook his head. "Not directly. Directly you measure other things, small things, things that you have at hand, and from them you work—*by reasoning*—to the Sun, ninety-three million miles away."

Even if Ralph was right—and he sounded right—there was still something ridiculous in going on and on like an encyclopedia about the chicken wire used in Mr. Kinapi's dog kennel.

But George said to me: "For that Ralph, everything, everything is newsworthy. The lint in your belly button is newsworthy. What you had for lunch three years ago is newsworthy. He is crazy, I tell you, and gives me all the day a headache." With a large brown finger he tapped the aspirin bottle next to the framed picture of his two young children.

I had been working for about a week when I

began noticing the sabotage. When Ralph stepped out for a minute to go to the bathroom, one of the reporters, thinking that no one was looking, went to Ralph's desk and removed a page from the middle of a thick manuscript. A practical joke, I thought. Later in the day, Ralph scratched his head and frowned, just like an Earthman.

A bottle of India ink was emptied in his drawer. A whoopee cushion was placed on the seat of his chair. (Sitting, he jumped and uttered a stifled curse in what must have been the Caraputanian tongue.) A dead cat was found, stiff, in his folded umbrella.

But some of the misbehavior was directed not at the alien personally: the paper itself seemed to be the target. Someone went around and put chewing gum inside all the typewriters.

(Oddly, Mr. Mtimkulu was not at all angered by these pranks. He even took enjoyment, I thought, in relating them to others. Was this sort of thing a tolerated custom here?)

The few times I tried to question Ralph about his race and home planet, he said that he was in a hurry and couldn't stop to chat. There was too much for him to learn. Once I trotted alongside as he rushed to cover some story (having to do with an upcoming trade agreement with the Malagasy Republic), and asked him why knowledge was that important to him. "Is it because knowledge is power?" I asked, panting.

He was listening to me with only half an ear, absorbed in his notebook, which he held before him as he ran and in which he even managed to jot a few words—when ideas came to him—while dodging between the people in the street and the lampposts. "Power?" he said. "What power?"

"Knowledge is power."

"Oh. No." He shook his head emphatically. "For us, knowledge is knowledge."

And that was the most I was able to get out of him.

The five-part feature that he did on the archaeological digs in Mashonaland was so impressive that a Harare publisher wanted to put it out in book form, with color plates. (Mr. Mtimkulu should have been pleased by this coup over Nyikadzinashe, but he made a pained face whenever the subject came up.) Also, Ralph uncovered a great deal of government corruption. Unfortunately, most of it was at too high a level and had to be hushed up.

I received a letter from Bea. It was full of resolves for the future, self-improvement, education, and career, and every other line hinted at marriage. "It's time I got serious," she wrote, "and did some planning with my life, if I'm to take care of myself. We have to be realistic." The stationery was pink and perfumed.

How the world would end became clear to me one bleak, windy Friday morning. I was getting over a stomach virus, still a little weak in the legs but glad to be up and about again. On my way to work I saw a gray-haired woman planting flowers in a window box. Framed by her window, she wore a red kerchief and held a trowel. The flowers, yellow and purple, glistened with water. The woman moved slowly and deliberately, in the way of old people, her face knitted in concentration.

A Caraputanian, passing by, looked at the flowers and remarked, with a nod, "Oh, *Viola tricolor hortensis*. Very European."

The old woman stopped. When the alien was gone, she lifted her trowel, bent over, and silently unearthed the flowers and dropped them, one by one, into the street.

So I wasn't taken completely by surprise when, at the paper, I found George (of all people) urinating into the trash can. When he saw me, he grinned sheepishly, like a kid caught in the act of writing "fuck" on a wall with a piece of chalk. "This, I always wanted to do," he whispered, giggling. The room reeked for the remainder of the day, even though we removed the trash can and used a scented aerosol. George was unrepentant: whenever I looked at him, he was shaking with mirth at his desk.

Remembering my experience in Ohio, the difficulty I had had with the paycheck when the Öht influence took over, I went to Mr. Mtimkulu and asked for all my wages and a small loan, to cover the airplane ticket. I promised that I would reimburse him as soon as I got back to the States.

"What a shame," he said. "There is illness in your family?"

"Yes," I said, not untruthfully.

Mr. Mtimkulu sighed. "We could use you now, Wally, the little jokes you make with the English, the expressions. We need things to be . . . lighter. But family, of course, must come first." He shook my hand and took me down to Payroll, where I signed a couple of papers and received the money.

Frumzig, fortunately, was not in sight when I hurried out, so I was spared that handshake. Nor did I bother to pick up my few belongings at his mother's: I knew by now that the infection spread rapidly once it began.

Ralph was coming the opposite way, returning from another successful (I did not doubt) in-the-field investigation.

"A word of warning," I said to him.

"For *me*?" He was interested.

"Yes. The pranks that they have been playing on you may get uglier. Your life, even, may be in danger."

"Really?" His Caraputanian eyebrows went up.

"The people here, on this planet, you see, don't like to be made to feel inferior."

Ralph was not sympathetic. "The world, you know, Walter, is given to us as it is. I am not to blame for someone else's inferiority." After this brief philosophical exchange—and rare, I believe, for the Caraputanians, who preferred hard fact to opinion or abstraction—he continued quickly on his way, not in the least afraid. (Possibly he carried an extraterrestrial weapon.)

I was wrong about the danger to him. Humanity did not attack the aliens. A resentful adolescent does not attack (usually) his adult parent. He is sullen, given to occasional, impulsive displays of defiance. If there is any destruction involved, chances are that he himself will be the victim of it, not the parent.

Incidents of misbehavior were minor, and few and far between, as I headed for the airport. I saw someone litter. I saw a young girl take a gas cap off a car and put it in her pocket. That was all.

At the airport in Newark, twenty-four hours later, I experienced the urge to steal a roll of peppermint Life Savers at a newsstand. Possibly that was only because I was so foggy in the head from lack of sleep.

But the next day, after I had slept, the wicked thought came to me, in bed, before I even opened my eyes, not to pay back Mr. Mtimkulu. He could hardly get at me from the other side of the globe, and what difference did it make, anyway, really, if we were all going to be defunct in a month or two? In the meantime I had more use for the five hundred dollars than he did. With five hundred dollars I could buy a top-quality ten-speed bicycle. I could take rides in the park. (Everything was in bloom now.)

Of course I did nothing of the kind. First thing that morning, I put a check in an envelope and walked it to the post office, to make sure. There were two Caraputanians on the corner, getting information about something, but I ignored them.

Lucille was in when I phoned. Her response to the news of the end of the world was not what I would have expected. "Well, Wally, maybe it's a good thing," she said. "I can't say that we've improved the planet any. Maybe whatever replaces us—ants or frogs—will do a better job of it." She invited me over to her place for a kind of bon voyage party. The aphids that clustered around the holes of the receiver all turned and hissed at me in unison.

Lucille's apartment building downtown was fancy. Big potted plants, vines, made the lobby look like a jungle; there were halls with dark marble walls, and the moving pointers over the elevator doors were brass.

"Wally," she said, greeting me with a kiss, "your hands are like ice."

She wore a flimsy, small dress that showed off most of her legs and shoulders, and her hair was different. I couldn't help staring.

We drank a toast, with bubbling champagne, to the human race. Pulling me by the hand, she led me into her bedroom. I didn't tell her that there was a giant white slug on the bed—and she wouldn't have been interested. "This is it," I said to myself, heart pounding. The fulfillment of my wildest dreams. I had always been in love with Lucille. But the love-making itself turned out to be anything but romantic. It was practically the opposite of romantic. Bestial.

Bea asked me over for a long talk the following day. She was pale, earnest to the point of grimness, as we sat together on the couch. I listened patiently for at least an hour—she was telling me about her breakdown—but then the humorous idea came to me suddenly to be bestial with her, as Lucille had been with me.

When she was in the middle of a particularly involved, hesitant sentence, I—saying nothing—pulled at her blouse, making the buttons pop off. Bea did a certain amount of gasping and arm swinging, but then told me in a weepy whisper that she loved me dearly, had always loved me dearly, from the moment she first set eyes on me, at the soda fountain. She was very emotional. Unfortunately, what I did to her then had nothing really to do with the emotions.

Bea seemed to realize this after a while. Deeply wounded, she summoned up a sarcastic smile. The effect was disfiguring. I told her that she should be careful and keep her door locked at all times, because there would be a lot of lawlessness soon, on a scale that we hadn't seen since the Huns.

Back at my house, preparing for bed, I looked in the bathroom mirror and was shocked by the animal face that faced me. It was reality, no hallucination. With fangs and bristles I would have made a good Mr. Hyde.

Curtain Call

I had a dream in which Mrs. Evans, Mrs. Collins, Mrs. Merkle, and Aunt Penny were sitting around a long conference table. They were discussing me. "He has no one to talk to, now," said Aunt Penny. "He's as solitary as an oyster."

I can always talk to Mr. Tribovich, I thought, although lately I hadn't seen him in his backyard. Was he sick?

There were all kinds of diseases, these days. You couldn't tell whether a disease was from the Öht, as in the case of the sleeping sickness that broke out in the south of the planet and spread north (compliments of the rock-lion-polyps), or due to the general breakdown in our utilities and services, etc. Just drinking the water was taking a chance, and there hadn't been fresh vegetables for months.

I never cared for vegetables, but I knew their value now. I saw some lettuce in an abandoned garden a few blocks away and wolfed it down, dirt, bugs, and all.

Mr. Tribovich had a fit when in the middle of the night somebody plundered his vegetable garden.

Even the flowers were taken. I could understand it—
I had had half a mind to plunder the garden myself.
It was only Mr. Tribovich's size that held me in check.
A neighbor is a neighbor, but food is food. (But, also,
he had helped me douse the fire started by the bandits
when I refused to open the door to them. It did make
sense for us to try to stick together.)

"He should marry," said Mrs. Evans with a smile,
in my dream.

But marriageable women didn't show themselves
these days. They would be crazy to. I had no idea
how Bea and Lucille were faring. I avoided thinking
about them. Bandits captured a young thing across
the street and tortured her in public for hours. I went
down to the basement, finally, not to hear her screams
and pleading. I don't like the basement. Full of spiders
and the smell of mold, it depresses me.

The dream ended with a bad smell. Something
was burning. I got up quickly and checked the house.
No, the smoke was from outside. Every day, there was
smoke in the air, in the sky—not unlike the old times
when the factories were running and you had to hold
your nose going through Linden and Elizabeth.

I ate a little raw spaghetti for breakfast, got my
slingshot, inspected it, and went out rat hunting. It
was not fun, this having to hustle for protein every
minute of the waking day, with no opportunity to sit
and think. Most of all I missed the radio, the talk
shows. Those warm, relaxed voices used to take some
of the edge off the loneliness.

Frankenstein was waiting for me on Ninth Avenue. We often went rat hunting together. He is my
first repeated and persistent hallucination. I have begun to consider him company. (Does this mean that
I have finally gone bonkers?)

"Hello, Frank," I said. "Where do we look today?"

With a large, gray, cadaverous finger he pointed in the direction of the highway. Good idea: the drainage ditches around a cloverleaf, with the tall weeds and rainwater, made a likely spot. If we didn't get rats, we might get frogs or snakes.

We crossed a field on our bellies—no sense letting bandits see us (see *me*, that is, because of course they can't see Frankenstein, who isn't there). Twice I had narrowly escaped being murdered by bandits. Murder for them was entertainment. Perhaps because there is little else to do. Little to rob. My most valuable possessions are the elastic piece of my slingshot and my shoes (purchased in Ohio, remember?), which are still in good condition. (Also, in a pinch, leather is edible.)

Near the cloverleaf we were attacked by mosquitoes. I wondered what the mosquito view of the world was and how it differed from that of Siphon and Pulex, but sans peripheral it was not possible to engage insects in conversation. They were all over me, whining their mosquito whine; I swatted. Frankenstein was oblivious to the bites as we waded through the tall grass. Being a figment has its advantages.

We saw a big rat, black, on one of the concrete slopes beneath the overpass. He must have been ten pounds at least. I pulled out the slingshot and took a couple of stones from the ammunition pouch at my belt. Crouching low, we advanced. With a slingshot you have to get close.

The rat lifted his head, sniffed the air. You never could tell, with rats. Sometimes they stayed put, fearless, and sometimes they had the sense to scuttle for cover. This one was a scuttler, I thought, but just then there was a loud whoosh and whir above the overpass, and the rat, surprised, lifted his head again, giving me a perfect shot.

I didn't hesitate, although we were not as close as I would have liked. In my experience, when you shoot from too far, even if you get a direct hit, the force isn't sufficient. But perfect shots were rare and momentary and it was unthinkable to pass one up. I put as much as I could into the shot, and shot well. Frankenstein clasped his hands in excitement when the big rat fell over.

Cheering, we rushed to kill him. Stones only stunned the rats, or occasionally broke a leg; after a few seconds a rat would be back on his feet and into the underbrush for good. I stumbled in a culvert, in water, but Frankenstein righted me. The rat was no longer in sight. When we reached the bridge, however, we saw him struggling to disappear behind the skeleton of a bush. I shot again—and hit him again. This was a good day. I laughed and kissed the sling-shot.

No problem opening his throat with the kitchen knife. He turned and bared his teeth, of course, but was stilled with a kick. A month ago, before I learned how to do this, I always got my hands bitten. (I have scars.)

I gave the rat to Frankenstein to hold, and walked around the slope to the top of the overpass to see what the noise was. For some reason I thought that it might be a Red Cross helicopter. I kept hoping, I suppose, that there still were small pockets of civilization in existence and that eventually people would come around and start putting everything back to normal. Then we could all eat at McDonald's again.

But the thing that had made the whoosh and the whir, and was now landed in the center of the highway above the cloverleaf, lights blinking, was a spaceship. Another Öht invasion, I said to myself. A bit late, this one. But no, people were getting on, not getting off. They were Caraputanians.

"Wait!" I called out. "Where are you going?"

The last Caraputanian, his foot on the step, looked back at me.

I ran up to talk to him. But I had difficulty catching my breath. The running and shouting weakened me. With so little protein available, these days, one can't exert oneself too much. "You're not leaving us, are you?" I asked.

"Yes," replied the Caraputanian.

"Why? Oh—I guess things aren't as interesting here for you now."

The alien shook his head. "We've done this planet."

"Filled up your notebooks, you mean? And now you have other planets to do?"

"That's it," said the Caraputanian, nodding. "Bye."

And before I knew it, there was a big wind as the ship rose, and a cloud of dust. It knocked me over, and I must have bumped my head on something then, because I had a dream. I dreamt that I was at a party. It was an enormous gathering, and yet I knew every person there. Waiters and waitresses moved gracefully in and out among the guests with trays of hors d'oeuvres; everyone held a glass of the most expensive French champagne, even the animals, and the chandeliers gleamed like upside-down trees of diamonds.

I mingled. Dr. Gross was talking to a macramé. "We are redefining the whole concept of insanity," he said. The macramé stifled a yawn and said, "On D'de, there are more than eight thousand distinct forms of insanity, but, curiously, fewer than eight thousand inhabitants."

Corporal Cimick (the bedbug, remember?) clinked his glass with Frumzig's mother. They seemed to be getting along well together, though neither spoke.

Mrs. Sanders, giggling, leaned over as she listened to a whispered joke told by a green gourd. "Oh, that's *filthy*," she said, looking a lot younger than when I knew her as a nurse at Rosedale.

Arms around each other, Donald Duck and Tolya sang by the piano, while Mr. Bostwick played. The song was in Russian and very hearty, in places sounding more like laughter than a song. Tolya waved his arms operatically, and Mr. Bostwick beamed. "What a nice group," I thought.

Off in a corner, the urbane police interrogator from Harare was having a heated political discussion with a toucan. "But you must realize," he was saying, "that there *is* no real proletariat in Peru." The toucan shook its long beak in disagreement.

And a penguin, at a glass table in another corner, was teaching old Mr. Forbes how to play checkers. They were too absorbed to notice the food.

Then someone clapped his hands and got the Öht to do a dance routine, in a sort of chorus line. They were all there, my five opponents, my five invaders, who threatened and finally destroyed mankind with demoralization. But that was spilt milk, water under the bridge.

As widely different as they were, they danced in perfect step, and I saw for the first time that they were really all the same. The lascivious gourd was the same as the aesthetic file cabinet with the camera eyes. The novelty-seeking clump of string was no different from the odd pyramidal chimera who only asked for a place to rest. And the superstudent with the notebook could have substituted for any of the above.

Because suddenly I knew what the word "Öht" meant. The Öht were not seeking or collecting, or out to obtain—they were really fleeing. They were fleeing a thing that was within. "Öht," in fact, in the Bayfí language, was the reflexive of flight. And when I saw the object—the subject, rather—of that reflexive, I couldn't blame them. It was the hardest reality of all, and the closest, to every creature in the universe.

And all flight from it was, ultimately, in vain.

It grinned at me.

In my dream, I sighed. The sigh came out more forcefully than I intended. It swept the Öht away, in the middle of their dance, like dandelion fluff. Actually, I wasn't sighing but coughing—from the dust in the air. I sat up on the highway and rubbed my temples. The dream loosened its hold on me, and with it went the profundity.

I got to my feet and looked down the highway in both directions: empty, all lanes, from horizon to horizon. I remembered the rat, and hurried back across the slope to Frankenstein, who was faithfully shooing away the bluebottles and botflies for me.

An unusually heavy rat. It had probably got into some farmer's storage bin and eaten itself silly. The weight was what had slowed it down. I offered to share the spoils with Frankenstein, but he declined like the gentleman he was. (But if he was real and not imagined, I *still* would have offered to split the rat with him.)

We carried our prize to the creek, to skin it and clean it. The creek was between an old brick building, long and windowless, and a barbed-wire fence. Beer cans, roofing material, and automobile tires lay on the sides and in the water, but the water was as clear and sweet-smelling as you could want: it had purged itself of all the chemicals. (The environmentalists would be pleased.)

Frankenstein helped me arrange the rat on our flat skinning rock. Skinning animals takes a while and is a lot of work—more work than it used to be, since the kitchen knife is getting duller and I haven't found a sharpener yet. I cut off the rat's head. The head, instead of floating away or sinking when I tossed it into the creek, remained in place on the surface, as if treading water. It opened its eyes and looked at me.

"Do you see what I see, Frank?" I said. My hallucinations, bless their heart, still had the ability to surprise.

But Frankenstein, incredibly, nodded. He saw it, too.

Not a hallucination, then?

A thrill of hope went through me. If it wasn't a hallucination, then it could be a messenger from the Conservationists themselves. And about time, I thought. The Conservationists could get us out of this mess. They could give me another peripheral (or recharge the old one). I crossed my fingers.

"Are you from the Conservationists?" I asked the head.

"Keep your voice down, Mr. Griffith," said the head of the black rat. The creek water swirled tranquilly around and past it. "I don't believe we're being observed, but there's no point in taking chances."

I looked over my shoulder, but saw no sign of those whose attention is best avoided. There was only the old brick wall and the weeds.

I approached the creek, squatted at the edge, as

if resting, and kept my eyes on an object—a rusted eggbeater—a good ninety degrees from the emissary. (Couldn't it have found something nicer to talk from?) Out of the corner of my mouth I said:

"Let's get right to the point. Would you tell the Conservationists please to reverse this end of the world?"

"End of the world?" said the rat's head, lifting its eyebrows.

I indicated the surroundings with a sweep of my hand. "You can see for yourself."

"The world is still here."

"I mean the end of the world in the sense of the end of the human race." This emissary seemed dense.

"It's because of the Öht," said the head.

"I *know* that. We've had one wave of them after another."

"They always come in waves."

"Yes, well, we held them off for a while," I said, "but then more than one invasion started coming at the same time. It wasn't fair—I'm only one person. Isn't there a rule against simultaneous invasions?"

"There isn't," said the head, "and please don't raise your voice."

I realized, with a cold sinking in my stomach, that the emissary hadn't come to help. "What are you here for?" I asked.

"Monitoring. I will report back."

"And you'll report that we've lost? That we're not the lucky 'one out of ten'?"

"That's correct."

"Look, can't the Conservationists make an exception in our case?" I stole a glance at the head, saw its whiskers and pointed nose. The beady eyes contained no sympathy.

But I had to make an appeal. Perhaps I would hit on a successful argument.

"Look," I said, fixing my eyes back on the egg-beater, "the Conservationists could intervene *a little*. They're so powerful, it wouldn't even raise a sweat on them, to help us. And you-know-who would never know. What would be the harm in it?"

No response from the head.

"All we need is a second chance. To be put on our feet again. We'd take it from there."

Still nothing.

"I guess you're not aware of this, but humanity has produced great art, architecture, works of music. We produced Beethoven. Leonardo da Vinci. Have you ever been to a museum or a concert?"

No response.

"Great things could come of us in the future. A lot of good. Who knows? But we need a future, to find out."

No response.

"Won't the Conservationists *feel* bad if they don't help? If they turn their backs on us? Letting all that potential for good go down the drain? I know they care. If they didn't care, they wouldn't have come in the first place and made me a guardian and given me the peripheral."

Silence.

"I wasn't the best guardian, true. But that was *my* fault. Blame me, don't blame the people of Earth. *They* shouldn't be punished."

Nothing.

"There are billions, billions of people over the globe. (There are fewer now, but never mind.) And each person has his own hopes and dreams. There are families, there is love. We have saints, builders, entertainers. All that doesn't deserve to be erased with a snap of the fingers."

The head said: "I have to go, Mr. Griffith. It may console you to consider, first of all, that some civilizations do manage to avert or repulse the Öht. Think of them as continuing in your stead, or carrying on the flame. Second, the Earth remains existent, the ecosystem intact, and evolution in operation. A few million years from now—which is a mere blink in the grand panorama of time—there is bound to be a civilization of some sort flourishing here on your native soil."

"Yes, based on wombats," I muttered. "Look, couldn't I speak to the Conservationists directly?"

But the head was gone. There were a few bubbles where it had been, on the surface of the water. The current bore the bubbles away.

"Well, we tried," I said to Frankenstein. He shrugged.

The skinning of the rat took more than half an hour. We were careful to keep washing the blood off. At the smell of blood, all sorts of pests pop up. Bugs, mainly. Flies and creeping things. I wasn't concerned about carnivores, such as dogs; there were not that many dogs left, and the ones left generally didn't cause trouble. (A week ago, in Roselle Park, I saw a poodle on a street corner, a skinny, muddy creature with bald patches. As soon as it saw me, it ducked, as if a brick had been hurled at it, and scooted out of sight.)

Frankenstein wrapped the rat carcass in a piece of green lawn bag that he had found and folded away for future use. (He was highly resourceful, an ideal companion on an outing. I knew, for example, that we would have no problem getting a fire started, even though we were out of matches and lighter fluid.)

We carried the rat to a field that once served as a school baseball diamond. This was where we usually cooked our meals, using bits of dry-rotted wood from the bleachers for fuel. The visibility was good in every direction, so no one could sneak up on us while we ate.

Apropos of nothing, I had another dream. (Not healthy, this sudden dreaming. What if a dream hit me in the middle of something important, such as running from bandits or taking aim at a rat?) This dream was biblical: Earth visited by ten plagues. The plagues were not clearly defined, but all were unpleasant and had something to do with the skin. The situation was made more difficult by the fact that the power was out.

"Christ," said a friend of mine. He was sitting in a chair, in the dark, scratching furiously. "We can't even watch television, for distraction."

The air conditioning didn't work, either.

"And the food in the refrigerator will spoil," someone remarked.

"No, don't open it," called a thin voice when I reached for the door of the refrigerator. "The smell will make us ill."

But I was so tremendously hungry—I couldn't remember the last time I had had a full meal—that I could have eaten anything, no matter how spoiled, rancid, rotten.

When I opened the door, a strong smell hit me. But the smell was really not that bad. In fact, when you got used to it, it was not bad at all. My mouth watered. I opened my eyes and saw Frankenstein bending over the fire. He had the rat on a spit already and was turning it.

Roasted rat: out of this world. The aroma, however, brought guests. I should have run for cover, but I was just too hungry. I drew my kitchen knife instead—a poor excuse for a weapon, but I was not about to part with this feast. There were three of them, three bandits, the most miserable, bedraggled bandits I had ever met, in worse shape even than the poodle in Roselle Park.

"What do you want?" I said. It came out in a snarl.

The one in the middle licked his lips and said hoarsely, "Smells good."

I nodded. Would they attack? But they seemed too weak and weary even to think of such exertion. One of them walked painfully, with a crutch; one had his head wrapped in a gray rag that served as a bandage. I saw that the hands of the one in the middle were trembling. These poor bastards were at least as hungry as I. Perhaps they did not even have the luxury of raw spaghetti in the morning. I felt pity.

"Maybe . . . we could have the bones," suggested the one with the head bandage, in a very faint voice. The other two looked at me, stooped, with big eyes, begging.

Times had to be pretty hard, I thought, if bandits were brought so low. I could picture them slavering noisily over the bones, gnawing at the tendons, and sucking for all they were worth to get out the marrow—whatever marrow a rat had.

I kneeled, cut off the little legs, and passed them around. The bandits, speechless, looked at me as if I were a god. "Don't worry," I told them. "There's more where this came from."

We polished off the rat in a few minutes. Frankenstein looked on with pleasure, like an uncle watching greedy children open their Christmas presents.

While we lay around the coals dozing and burping, I showed the bandit leader my slingshot. He was impressed. I told him about the other slingshots I had tried but which didn't work because there was no good elastic. The stones would bounce off the rat and the rat would practically laugh in my face. But as soon as I found the good elastic, I began acquiring protein.

The bandit sighed. Protein was the big problem. "We can't live off the grass, like cows," he said.

(Cows had to be extinct by now.)

The three of them, he said, had tried eating shoe leather, from a find in a dump across the highway—the shoe stores having long since been cleaned out—but their teeth weren't up to it. Teeth would come loose, probably because of the lack of vitamin C. "And teeth you can't replace," said the bandit. He smiled wide to show me what he meant. I tsk-tsk'ed in sympathy. Big gaps, top and bottom.

My guests admired my shoes from Ohio.

Would they attempt to kill me now that they had a little strength from the meat? My elastic and my shoes were double cause for murder. But no, these bandits were all gratitude. They thanked me a hundred times for sharing my rat with them. And they were glad for the opportunity to talk. And I was glad, too. Although Frankenstein makes a fine companion, he never says a word (which isn't his fault).

We talked until dusk, not once mentioning the old times. The smoke-filled sky over the baseball field glowed a beautiful deep red as the sun went down.

ABOUT THE AUTHOR

MICHAEL KANDEL is an editor, writer, translator. He lives on Long Island, New York, with a chemist wife and two sons, and daily braves the Long Island Railroad to work at a major hardcover publisher in Manhattan. He has been nominated twice for the National Book Award for his translations of Stanislaw Lem. This is his first novel.

Spectra Special Editions

Bantam Spectra Special Editions is a program dedicated to masterful works of fantastic fiction by many of today's most visionary writers. Don't miss them!

☐ **Out on Blue Six** (27763-4 • $4.50/$5.50 in Canada) by Ian McDonald. On the run in a society where the state determines one's position in life, Courtney Hall takes charge of her fate, turning from model citizen to active rebel.

☐ **The Nexus** (27345-2 • $4.50/$5.50 in Canada) by Mike McQuay. The tale of an autistic girl who can literally work miracles and the reporter who brings her story to the world.

☐ **Memories** (28067-8 • $4.95/$5.95 in Canada) by Mike McQuay. Winner of the Philip K. Dick Special Award. An embittered psychologist travels through time to preserve the fabric of reality.

☐ **Phases of Gravity** (27764-2 • $4.50/$5.50 in Canada) by Dan Simmons. An ex-astronaut goes on a personal odyssey to centers of power all over the earth in search of an elusive—but powerful—fate he senses awaiting him.

☐ **Strange Toys** (26872-4 • $4.50/$5.50 in Canada) by Patricia Geary. Winner of the Philip K. Dick Award. A young woman tries to come to grips with the supernatural powers that pervade her life.

☐ **Unicorn Mountain** (27904-1 • $4.95/$5.95 in Canada) by Michael Bishop, author of the Nebula Award-winning **No Enemy But Time.** When unicorns appear on a Colorado mountain, four people must overcome their own frailties to save the unicorns from exctinction.

Buy Spectra Special Editions wherever Bantam Spectra Books are sold, or use this handy page to order:
